FAMILY
TIES

ALSO BY GARY PAULSEN

GARY PAULSEN

FAMILY TIES

The Theory, Practice, and Destructive Properties of Relatives

A YEARLING BOOK

Text copyright © 2014 by Gary Paulsen
Cover art copyright © 2014 by James Bernardin

All rights reserved. Published in the United States by Yearling, an imprint of Random House Children's Books, a division of Random House LLC, a Penguin Random House Company, New York. Originally published in hardcover in the United States by Wendy Lamb Books, an imprint of Random House Children's Books, New York, in 2014.

Yearling and the jumping horse design are registered trademarks of Random House LLC.

Visit us on the Web! randomhousekids.com

Educators and librarians, for a variety of teaching tools, visit us at RHTeachersLibrarians.com

The Library of Congress has cataloged the hardcover edition of this work as follows:
Paulsen, Gary.
Family ties / by Gary Paulsen. — First edition.
pages cm
Summary: " 'I'm the greatest family member you'll ever meet.' Kevin Spencer has a history of big ideas going completely awry. This time around, it's personal—suddenly he's kind of in charge of a double wedding in his backyard, and a whole tribe of wacky relatives is crowding him out of his own house"—Provided by publisher.
ISBN 978-0-385-37380-7 (hardback) — ISBN 978-0-385-37381-4 (lib. bdg.) — ISBN 978-0-385-37382-1 (ebook) [1. Family life—Fiction. 2. Interpersonal relations—Fiction. 3. Weddings—Fiction. 4. Humorous stories.] I. Title.
PZ7.P2843Fam 2014
[Fic]—dc23
2013025829

ISBN 978-0-385-37383-8 (pbk.)

Printed in the United States of America

10 9 8 7 6 5 4 3 2 1

First Yearling Edition 2015

*This book is dedicated to the memory of
Erin Copeland and to her parents,
Beverly and Sheldon Copeland,
who created the Erin Copeland Building Minds
with Books Project to share Erin's love of reading
with people who might not have had
books of their own.*

Foreword

I'm the greatest family member you'll ever meet.

I should be good; growing up in a home like mine, I've had to contend with a whole lot of dysfunctionality, which if it isn't a word should be. To paraphrase some great spiritual leader, I had to become the family unity I wanted to see. I'm only fourteen, but my family has always been able to depend on me to bring us all together. It's a universal rule. A cosmic inevitability.

At least, it is in the House of Spencer.

If you ask me, people who aren't close to their families are just lucky. No, just kidding; I'm a kidder. Ba dum bump. Having a sense of humor is important when you're the leader of a family. Mom and Dad might disagree about who has that title, officially, but everyone knows that Kev's the one the Spencers turn to when they're facing a crisis. Like when they can't remember the code to the security alarm. Our code is 53846. I've got a great memory for numbers; plus, the code spells KEVIN. No one else has figured that out.

They'd be lost without me.

My ability to draw people closer together is a gift. I must have been born with a few extra instincts to preserve the tribe. See, people like to feel they belong somewhere, and I'm good at making sure that happens. I'd have done even better in prehistoric times, when everyone lived and slept in caves, huddled together for warmth and protection.

From the day I was born, baby number three, I've been the glue that holds the Spencers together. Everyone knows odd numbers are more visually pleasing than even ones. Plus, Dad and Daniel needed me to offset Mom and Sarah.

No one else takes the time to talk with everyone the way I do. Even though they accuse me of snooping, prying and gossiping, everyone goes through me to get the scoop on what the other Spencers are up to. Even Auntie Buzz, who has lived in the apartment over our garage for as long as I can remember.

I'm easily the most popular member of my family. Mom and I sit around the table and share news a few evenings a week. Dad and I challenge each other with sports facts and stats as we hand each other pieces of the newspaper over breakfast, the highest form of male-to-male communication. Daniel and I are allies against Sarah, and everyone knows a shared enemy is the tightest connection. And even Sarah and I have a mutual respect—we both think we're the smartest person we know and that we're each other's only competition for that title.

I'm practically raising Markie, my four-year-old neighbor. Teddy, our cat, sleeps on the foot of my bed. Small children and pets are excellent judges of character because they're dependent creatures; they've learned to spot good people in order to survive.

As for my friends, I'm the sun to their planets. I'm the one who introduced my buddies Wheels and Dash to each other and then to my best pal, JonPaul; Katie Knowles and Connie Shaw wouldn't be friends if they hadn't known me first; and JonPaul's cousin Goober found his girlfriend, Betsy, with an assist from me. Because I care. And I understand the innate need to connect.

When I grow up, my girlfriend, Tina, and I will

have a huge family—lots of kids, maybe a bunch of foreign exchange students and a ton of pets. Tina doesn't know this yet. But I just know our house will be the one where everyone celebrates the holidays and argues about bad calls during the big game and stresses out over election results. "That Kevin," they'll all say. "He brings everyone together."

If you look at it the right way, I am the cherry on top of the Spencer family sundae.

I'm not bragging. I'm just saying.

See, I don't lie and I don't hustle for money and I don't set up my friends and family so I can study their reactions and I'm not trying to run the school.

Not anymore.

I used to think like that. Until I wound up in the middle of so much drama that I looked into becoming a monk on monastery.com so I could live out the rest of my life in isolation. And silence.

Now I'm all about family.

1

The Normal Family Encourages Each Member to Make Big Plans for the Future

I'm the happiest guy alive. Because Katrina M. Zabinski is my girlfriend.

I'm also the most miserable guy who ever lived, because the pressure of having a girlfriend like Tina is crushing.

See, Tina's not just any girl; she's the universe's most astonishing specimen of female sublimity. She has hair that sparkles and skin that glows and blue-green eyes that twinkle. Glinda the Good Witch and her bubble look dull compared to Tina.

One thing I've noticed about the whole boyfriend-and-girlfriend thing is that there is a lot of breaking up.

But not me and Tina. No way.

It doesn't take a rocket scientist to see which one of us got the better deal here, and it wasn't her. When you're lucky enough to have found and then caught a girl like Tina, you worry. How do you make sure you're not going to lose her? Ever?

So far, Tina and I have had two dates, and they were both accidental. The first was when we ran into each other at a neighbor's party, and the second happened when she came by my house after I ran for class president. She helped me make good on some of my brilliant ideas.

Dates like that weren't going to show her that I'm a happily-ever-after, forever-and-ever kind of guy. Not just a middle school boyfriend, but a family man.

Go big or go home, I always say.

Other guys might be content with knowing their girlfriend is a lock until the next big party or school dance. Not me.

So I had to plan the Perfect Official First Date *and* figure out how to show Tina that she'd already met her lifelong significant other: Kevin Lucas Spencer.

I got my first clue on how to start before first period Friday, when I noticed she was upset. Her forehead was scrunched and she was having an intense whispered conversation with her best friend, Connie.

"And then I told him he was a terrible brother and that I was going to tell Mom what he called me!" The anguish in Tina's voice ripped at my heart.

Connie said something, but I didn't listen; I was waiting for it to be Tina's turn to talk again.

"You think?" Tina looked doubtful, which, on her, is adorable. "I mean, it would be nice if he said sorry first, but maybe trying to make things better is the right thing to do. My folks say we should be there for each other, no matter what."

The ideal girl—smoking hot *and* a great sister.

The bell rang, so I sat back to figure out how to use this information to my advantage.

Clearly, Tina values family. So do I. I figured if I could show her how much we had in common in that area, she'd have to see how indisputably Made for Each Other we were.

I knew I might have to fake my part a little bit. My family argues with each other all the time and no one ever rushes to apologize.

I was so caught up in thinking about getting Tina to see me as her future husband without freaking her out—we're only fourteen, and not everyone is willing to make a lifetime commitment at our age like I am—that I hardly heard a word of class. I looked like

I was taking notes, but I was really making a word search puzzle around Tina's and my names and words like *truelove* and *neverbreakingup* and *Deacon,* which is what I hope she'll agree to name our first dog.

As always, I died a little inside when Tina said goodbye at the end of class. I'd counted the minutes until our schedules would cross again (141). Facing that long a separation bummed me out, but I took a deep breath and headed to social studies, which I like.

Mr. Crosby started talking the second the bell rang.

"After the, uh, unexpected developments during the recent student body president campaign, it's clear that we should revisit the workings of the American political process.

"We are a nation claiming to believe in life, liberty and the pursuit of happiness for all." Crosby was trying to make eye contact with everyone. He acts like a spot check from the superintendent might happen at any time and he wants his classes to be caught in the middle of a learning miracle.

"And yet it is sometimes difficult to remain aware of our responsibility to listen to and learn from those who don't share our exact ideology."

That's what he said, but what I wrote in my notes

was *People don't pay attention to people they disagree with*. Summarizing is one of my academic strengths.

"When we perceive our fellow citizens as strangers rather than allies, we lose all sense of community and shared vision. We have a responsibility that we must exercise on behalf of our national, if not our global, human family."

Family. I leaned back and smiled.

"A family is, of course, a miniature replica of society itself. So that's why, next week"—Crosby rubbed his hands together like he couldn't wait for Monday to arrive—"we're going to break up into family units in class and work on problem solving vis-à-vis close familial relationships and situations. This will help you to become more politically sensitive."

Crosby had us read a chapter in our textbooks about, I don't know, support and compromise, for the remainder of the period. I skimmed the section and spent the rest of my time pondering: Should I take guitar lessons or a painting class? Which one would Tina want to do with me? Thinking about what's best for our relationship takes a lot of work, let me tell you.

At lunch, I sailed into the cafeteria ready for a sloppy joe and a pudding cup, starving from all the thinking and planning and lovelorn stuff.

I stopped. I smelled Tina.

She has . . . an aura that surrounds her. I think it's shampoo combined with her inner goodness. As soon as I catch my first whiff, my nose turns in its direction. My feet don't always get the message and, as usual, I walked into the doorframe before I could stop myself. I bounced off, and as soon as my vision cleared I found myself facing Tina, who was talking to Katie Knowles and Milania Zeman. Katie was our student body president, and Milania was our Top Girl Jock.

"I've been looking for you two all morning," Tina said to them, but smiled at me, pretending, as usual, that she hadn't seen me make an idiot of myself. That smile makes me wish I could slay a dragon or lift an FV623 Stalwart amphibious 6×6 five-ton artillery supply vehicle with my bare hands. Or even just walk without tripping.

Tina handed Katie a sheet of paper. "I wanted to give you my application for the Fine Arts Fair. I'm so excited for the opportunity to exhibit my sketches."

The ringing in my ears from my collision with the door turned into the sound of opportunity knocking.

"Count me in." My voice cracked, turning those three syllables into about twelve, but I didn't even care, because Tina smiled at me again before she floated off. Well, she got in line to buy her lunch, but she did it in such a light and graceful and smooth way that I wondered if she was part pixie. I looked down to see if she'd left a trail of glitter.

The part of me that reacts to Tina before the rest of me realizes what's going on turned to Katie and Milania, hoping they'd explain what I'd just signed up for. Not that I cared. I'd have volunteered for an allergy study where I was stuck with needles and observed for life-threatening reactions if it meant participating in an activity with Tina.

"The Fine Arts Fair is a joint task force between the student government and the athletics department," Katie told me.

No, I corrected her silently, it's just another way for Kevin to score additional points with the girl of his dreams.

Too bad it meant involvement with the two most intimidating girls I know. Life is never completely perfect.

Even though Katie and I have what could be called a complicated history, I'd recently seen glimmers that, if I could stop messing up and Katie could tone down the profoundly grating aspects of her personality, she and I just might make a good team. We were finally on the same page and trying to get along.

But I knew better than to push my luck with too many conversations, because I have this crazy tendency to take advantage of her if we hang around together.

Milania and I had crossed paths when, um—what do they say in the gangster movies?—when we cut a mutually advantageous deal after she made me an offer I couldn't refuse. She's not the kind of person you want on your bad side, so I was glad everything worked out, more or less, and we were friendly, more or less. Again, it was better not to push my luck by spending too much time with her.

If you ask me, avoidance is an overlooked and underappreciated tactic for keeping a friendship in good shape.

"It'll be an amazing accomplishment to list on our college applications in a few years," Katie told me. "You can never start too soon if you want to protect your future."

Exactly what I'd been thinking all morning. I was glad to know I wasn't the only one in this school with an eye on the big picture. Leave it to Katie to be thinking along the same lines as me.

"Uh-huh," I murmured, watching Tina pick out a milk carton. "When is it?"

"A week from tomorrow." Milania handed me an application, but when I looked at the sheet of paper, what I saw was Another Way for Kevin to Show Tina Theirs Is a Romance for the Ages. "What are you thinking of displaying? Painting, sculpture, photography, jewelry?"

"Yes," I answered absently. "That sounds great. Definitely." Tina was walking to her lunch table, so I couldn't really concentrate on what Milania was saying.

Sometimes it's so good to be me that I feel bad for everyone else.

2

The Normal Family Has an Open-Door Policy for All Members

Sunday nights are the best time of my whole week. That's when everybody goes to their rooms and shuts the doors because this is "drop everything and read" time at the Spencers'. We leave each other alone with our books and, in my case, a bowl of melted chocolate chips and a few bananas for dunking. It's the perfect way to prepare for the week ahead.

I'd had a busy weekend; I play lacrosse on Saturday mornings and then I have two jobs, and I'd spent Sunday obsessing about my plan to make Tina aware of my potential so that she'd never suffer the agony of looking back at me as the One That Got Away. Being as thoughtful as I am is surprisingly exhausting.

I'd just settled on my bed, cracked the spine of my book and started to peel the first banana when the doorbell rang. As always when someone showed up at the door, or my cell chirped, or my computer dinged with a message, I hoped it was Tina.

"Hey!" I heard my uncle, Will, bellow. "Sorry about knocking your mailbox off the side of the house when I reached to ring the bell. Didn't see it. Also didn't see the flowerpot I tripped on. Smashed. Man, it's like an obstacle course to get to your front door. You should do something about that."

The last time Dad's younger brother had visited us, he'd driven his car through the garage door, gotten arrested in our front yard for civil disobedience and left behind a swarming, wiggling mass of maggots under the kitchen sink after he missed the trash can with a half-eaten tuna-fish sandwich.

The garage door still doesn't work, Mom and Dad are worried that the neighbors blame them for giving the neighborhood a bad reputation, and none of us have been able to eat rice since Uncle Will left—I bet that's true of anyone who's ever been surprised by a colony of maggots.

Uncle Will was not guaranteed a warm welcome.

But Tina deserves a boyfriend who goes out of his

way to make things right between relatives, and fixing the Dad-not-speaking-to-Will situation seemed like a no-brainer. I had to prove to Tina that I, too, disliked familial discord and, just like her, was a force for good in sibling disagreements. But I never in a million years imagined that my harmless email to Uncle Will first thing this morning encouraging him to get in touch with Dad would lead to him showing up at our house.

All I'd done was tell Will that bygones should be bygones between family members. I'd just wanted to get Dad and Will *talking*.

Email is so ripe for misunderstanding.

And I should have remembered Uncle Will likes big gestures and surprises.

Too late now.

So I tiptoed across the room and pressed my ear against the door to hear better.

Then I dashed back to my bed to grab my snack, returned to the door and swirled the banana in the chocolate because it had started to congeal. Bananas are the perfect eavesdropping food—very quiet inside your head, unlike tortilla chips or carrot sticks.

"Michael!" Uncle Will's voice boomed. "Got a hug for your favorite brother?"

I guessed the answer was no. Correct that: No. Not. Ever.

After Will's last visit, Dad believes Will is somehow responsible for everything that bugs him, such as the Cubs' inability to get to the postseason and the sluggish Wi-Fi reception in the basement.

I cracked open my door and snuck a glance down the hall. Daniel and Sarah were peering out from their rooms too. Sarah claims she still has nightmares about watching Will get handcuffed and taken away in a patrol car as her boyfriend, Doug, dropped her off after a date. Daniel blames Will for the fact that we spray so much disinfectant that his eyes water every time he enters the kitchen. And since the automatic garage door opener hasn't been repaired, I'm the one who has to open and close the door. Like in the olden days before electricity.

Sarah caught our eyes and gestured to us like the soldier in a war movie leading his platoon behind enemy lines. She inched down the hall to a vantage point where she could see the entryway. Daniel and I silently crawled after her.

We peeked around the corner and saw an awkward huddle in the entry. Mom and Dad wouldn't usually keep visitors standing at the door, but they were clearly

17

hoping that Will just wanted to say a quick hi on the front step and then leave.

But Uncle Will put his arm around a woman standing just outside the front door and pulled her into the house.

"This is Brandee. Spelled with two *e*'s. Because she's extra excellent."

"How do you do?" "Nice to meet you," Mom and Dad murmured, sounding doubtful. Brandee's extra excellence wasn't as obvious to my folks as it was to Uncle Will.

"Brandee's my new wife."

Before Mom and Dad could react, Uncle Will reached behind Brandee and yanked a small boy forward. He looked about Markie's age, maybe four or five years old.

"And this is her son, Larry. I call him Sparky. Sparky's going through that phase all young boys do where he's very curious about fire. So you want to keep him away from open flames, matches, flammable liquids, anything that might be used as kindling or has the potential to cause spontaneous combustion, the stove, the oven, the fireplace, the furnace, the water heater, the clothes dryer, pretty much anything with a pilot light."

"A pyro," Sarah whispered. Daniel and I nodded.

Uncle Will had saved the best for last. He reached behind Brandee again and pulled forth a polar bear on a leash.

"And this is Athena. Athena is part Great Pyrenees."

"The other part must be woolly mammoth," Daniel muttered.

"Isn't she a beaut?" Uncle Will's voice was filled with admiration.

All of a sudden, Mom screamed and Athena barked and someone bumped into the end table and the lamp fell over and crashed on the floor.

"Oh yeah," Will said cheerfully. "Athena's got a bladder infection. She can't always hold it real well."

Just then I caught sight of our cat, Teddy, poking his head out from beneath the couch. Weird—Teddy's not the friendliest cat you ever met and goes into invisibility mode when we have company. But something about Uncle Will, Brandee-with-two-*e*'s, Larry aka Sparky, and Athena, the incontinent crossbreed result of a fuzzy hippopotamus and a white SUV, piqued Teddy's curiosity.

Teddy crawled out to investigate and, no lie, did a perfect double take when he got a clear view of Athena. Then he arched his back and fluffed up

19

his tail and meowed, slinking over to wind between Athena's legs and rub his face on Athena's chest, purring loudly.

Sarah and Daniel and I looked at each other in shock. "Teddy's madly in love with Athena," I whispered, knowing just how he felt and hoping that I'd find a way to make this visit into a story that would impress and amaze Tina.

Athena must not have believed in love at first sight like Teddy, because she whined and tried to bolt from the house, yanking Uncle Will off his feet and halfway out the door. After a stumble when Athena tipped over the umbrella stand, which took out the coat rack, which knocked two pictures off the wall, Will braced himself against the doorframe and grabbed the leash with both hands. He won the tug-of-war and hauled Athena back inside.

Apparently, Athena's medical condition was exacerbated by thwarted attempts to escape, because she took another whiz on the entry floor.

That's when Sarah screamed "FIRE!"

She hurdled over Daniel and me and charged into the living room, heading for the fireplace. Sparky was trying to light a match and set the pile of logs and old newspapers alight.

Sarah body-checked Sparky hard enough to knock the matches out of his hands and send him sprawling on the floor.

Sarah might have learned enough as a hockey player's sister to do a good impression of an enforcer, but she didn't know how to account for momentum. After plowing into Sparky, she kept going. Straight into a cabinet full of Mom's collection of antique cups and saucers. The crash was deafening.

"Wow," I breathed.

"Yeah." Daniel shook his head. "That'd be a foul for sure on the ice, but nice technique—fast and low."

"She doesn't look hurt," I commented.

"Nah, she mighta got the wind knocked out of her, but she's not feeling any real pain. Once the adrenaline kicks in, you're pretty numb," Daniel explained.

Although Sparky had only managed to get one log smoldering, he hadn't opened the chimney flue, and the room smelled a little smoky. Just as that thought crossed my mind, Auntie Buzz came barreling out of the kitchen with the fire extinguisher. She squeezed the trigger, but the force of the spray must have caught her off guard, because the hose started spewing white powdery stuff all around the living room, nowhere near the fireplace.

After finally gaining control of the fire extinguisher, she said, "I smelled smoke."

"From your apartment over the garage?" Mom asked.

"No, from the kitchen. I saw Will's car from my window and had to see for myself what was going on. Jack and I snuck over and hid behind the door." She pointed to her boyfriend, who shyly waved from the kitchen.

"I appreciate your support," said Mom, rolling her eyes.

"That's what sisters are for." Buzz tended to miss sarcasm.

"Hey, Buzzy, I'd like you to meet my wife, Brandee." Will turned to his wife. "That's my sister-in-law's sister. She's nuts." He didn't seem to realize that Brandee wasn't the only person in the room who could hear him. Or that Buzz didn't take kindly to being called crazy by the man who'd once tried to set up a ferret-breeding farm.

Before Buzz could say anything, though, or introduce him to Jack, Athena yanked the leash out of Uncle Will's hand, jumped on the couch and stretched out. Teddy curled up next to her, and in a second, they were both snoring. Sometimes I take a nap when I can't think how else to avoid a tense situation too.

Will kept trying to edge farther into the living room, and Dad was trying to block him. Mom was looking from the broken lamp to the smashed pictures and then toward the shattered china cabinet. Brandee pulled tissues out of her purse and tried to sop up Athena's giant pee puddle. Buzz leaned against the doorframe and smirked, because usually she's the annoying relative making waves. Jack picked up Sparky and checked for injuries. Daniel grabbed the vacuum out of the hall closet, and Sarah started carefully picking shards of china out of the carpet. I filled a bucket with soapy water and then nudged everyone into the living room so I could start cleaning the floor.

The adults sat down, but they didn't say anything for the longest time, seeming to be fascinated by the Zamboni-like concentric circles my hockey-playing brother was making on the carpet with the vacuum cleaner.

"So, Will," Mom finally hollered over the roar of the vacuum. "You gave us a lot of information in a very short time. We're all so happy that you dropped by to share the, um, good news. DANIEL, CAN YOU PLEASE STOP DOING THAT RIGHT NOW?"

Daniel flipped the Off switch and the room was silent except for the white noise of Athena and Teddy snoring and the *scritch-scritch-scritch* of the scrubbing brush as I doggedly de-peed the entryway. Pun intended! Even in a crisis, I bring the funny.

"I couldn't wait to see your faces when I told you," Will said. "I had to tell you guys in person that Brandee is part of our family now. And Sparky. And Athena. Our family tree has three more branches!"

"Family is everything," I said from the floor, even though I suspected that Will had been more motivated by the drama of a small flash mob than the desire to share his news.

No one else said a word. Man, these people are never going to win any hospitality awards. I tried to compensate with an extra dose of friendly. "I wish we could have been at your wedding."

"I'm sorry about that," said Brandee, looking embarrassed. "It was a spur-of-the-moment ceremony, just us and the justice of the peace and two witnesses off the street. We didn't have family or friends with us."

"Bummer." Brandee and I nodded at each other. She looked so sweet and hopeful that she reminded me of Tina. I got inspired.

"You two should get married. Again. Because, of

course, you *are* married. But here. Like this weekend. So all of us can see it. I mean, as long as you're already here, it'd be great."

Brandee and Will grinned. "Well, maybe something small," Brandee said. "Casual and relaxed. I'm not really a big-fancy-wedding girl."

"Exactly, because all anyone needs for a kick-butt wedding is a cake, a white dress, a bow tie, a few presents. Geez, when you think about it, weddings practically throw themselves together," I said.

I. Am. Brilliant.

Dad tipped his head back and stared at the ceiling. Mom turned very pale and swayed in her chair; I thought for a second she might actually faint. Buzz, for probably the first time ever, beamed at Will, because after three and a half impulsive marriages of her own, they finally had something in common. Jack gave a fist pump. Sarah and Daniel looked totally bored with the whole scene; they aren't as eager to make sure everyone in their family is on good terms with each other as I am.

Sparky had fallen asleep on the couch, snoring along with Athena and Teddy.

"We should get him to bed," said Will. He picked Sparky up from the sleeping pack and looked around expectantly. "Long day, lots of excitement meeting his new relatives. Where do you want us?"

"Um . . ." Mom sounded doubtful. "I wasn't expecting houseguests tonight—and so many of you—I'm not sure how I should sort things. . . ."

"Oh, it's no worry. Don't put yourself out. We'll sleep anywhere. You'll hardly notice us," Will said, as if three guests and a ginormous pee-spraying dog could go unnoticed in anyone's house.

"How about the basement family room, on the couch that pulls out to a bed for you and Brandee, and the futon in the guest room for Sp—I mean Larry?"

Will made a face. "Small children shouldn't be in a basement where there might be mold. Besides, it would be really helpful if Sparky and Brandee and I shared one room with a door that locks. He tends to wander at night."

Mom got pale at the thought of Sparky's incendiary potential. "Hmm, let me think. . . ."

I've seen Mom stall before when she's hoping a problem will go away if she just waits it out, but I knew it wouldn't work here; Will never gets a hint and, besides, I was totally jazzed about them staying long enough for us to attend their wedding.

"There's only one solution," I blurted, avoiding

Mom's glare and pretending not to hear Dad swear under his breath. "I have a full-sized bed with a trundle. I don't have a lock, but you can move something heavy in front of the door so Sparky doesn't . . . wander. And I can go in Daniel's room, because he has bunk beds."

No one except Will looked happy, but Mom and Dad were too tired to discuss things any further. They seemed relieved to go to their room and shut the door.

Athena whined all night in the hallway, trying to get to Uncle Will and scratching at my bedroom door, which, while lock-free, did have my dresser shoved in front of it so Sparky couldn't investigate the mesmerizing lure of flames. Teddy wailed because his one true love was restless and unhappy. It was a long—and noisy—night.

But all things considered, it was one of the better starts to a visit by Uncle Will. At the very least, it was something none of us would ever forget. And memories are what bind a family together.

Tina would have to be crazy not to appreciate the lengths a guy like me will go to for the sake of family.

3

The Normal Family Thrives in an Atmosphere of Diversity and Tolerance

My grandmother showed up bright and early Monday morning. Correct that: Lucille showed up.

Dad's mom isn't the warm and cuddly, big smooshy hug, here-have-a-fresh-homemade-cookie granny type. In fact, Sarah, Daniel and I have to call her by her first name because she doesn't do the whole "Grandma" thing. Mom says we should be glad she doesn't make us call her Mrs. Spencer. Which, by the way, is what Mom calls her. Even though that's Mom's name too.

We hardly ever see Lucille. Because she's a pill. Weird to think we could even be related, given my warmth and charisma.

At any rate, Mom, Dad, Sarah, Daniel, Uncle Will, Brandee, Auntie Buzz and I had crammed into the kitchen for breakfast Monday morning. Sparky was under the kitchen table, either because that was the only space left in the room or because he was wadding the newspaper into kindling. Athena and Teddy had been put in the basement, where they were yowling and keening to be let out.

"You got married?"

We all looked up at the sound of Lucille's voice coming from the doorway.

"Mother. What are you doing here?" asked Will. Dad probably would have fallen over if he hadn't been jammed between Will and Daniel.

"I texted Lucille last night after you showed up," I jumped in. I didn't point out that no one else had even thought of contacting the groom's mother; that would have made everyone feel bad.

"You married a woman who has a small child?"

I was offended by her questions. Lucille hadn't believed my text? I'd given her all the info, including Sparky; no need to independently confirm the deets.

"I hit the jackpot, right? A prefab family." Will winked at Lucille. I'm pretty sure no one's ever winked

29

at her before, because she flinched and lost her train of thought for a second.

"They call him Sparky," I said helpfully.

"Because of his proclivity for starting fires?" Lucille glanced nervously at Sparky under the kitchen table.

"He keeps me on my toes." Will made it sound like being a potential firebug had been on his top ten list of stepson requirements.

"And you have a dog?" Lucille wasn't using her happy voice.

"How lucky am I?"

"You know how I feel about house pets." Lucille is a neat freak who disapproves of animals because they shed and "track in filth." Wait till she finds out about Athena's incontinence.

"Will and Brandee are going to renew their vows," I jumped in again, because this conversation wasn't headed in the direction I'd imagined when I texted Lucille the night before. "In the presence of our family."

Will grinned and threw his arm around Brandee's shoulders. He's got a knack for never noticing that he upsets people and so he's always calm and relaxed. I bet he never needs antiperspirant or aspirin or that pink acid-reducing stuff Dad drinks straight from the bottle when he's got a big presentation coming up.

"How are you going to support a wife and a stepson?" Lucille is such a killjoy.

"Don't forget Athena; between what she eats and her vet bills, she's easily the most expensive of all of us." Will beamed as if it was the greatest idea since gravity to have an expensive dog.

Lucille bent down and picked up the tiniest piece of pet fur from the floor. She held it as carefully as bomb squads handle unexploded devices. And then she tsked, which everyone knows is old-people language for words I'd get grounded for if I said out loud.

Mom, Dad, Sarah, Daniel, Auntie Buzz and I love Teddy, kind of, and Brandee and Uncle Will and Sparky love Athena, I suppose, and we're all a little on the slobby side. In that instant, as we watched Lucille dispose of the pet fur and then wash and sanitize her hands like she was heading into an operating room, we drew together in a tight bond, wordlessly agreeing to dislike her.

"Why was I the last to know?" Lucille demanded.

If the mere force of a shared idea could somehow

make thoughts audible, Lucille would have heard what everyone was thinking: because you're a buzzkill.

I wonder if she sensed that the room had turned against her, because she smiled. Well, she tried to smile. I don't think she gets a lot of practice.

"Where should I put my things?" Lucille asked, trying to act as if she hadn't gotten off on the wrong foot.

"You're staying here? With us?" Dad asked, and then lightly banged the back of his head against the fridge, already knowing the answer.

"Of course. It only makes sense."

Differential equations make sense; the laws that govern gravity and light in black holes make sense; the infield fly rule makes sense. Lucille staying here made zero sense.

I had NOT seen this coming when I texted her.

Why does NO ONE in this family respond with a simple phone call or a polite email? Tina and I, of course, will have a guest room that's always full of visitors. I just hope they have better manners than my relatives and wait to be invited.

Mom knows how to pick her battles and when to shift blame, so she looked at me. "Well, Mr. Vociferous, I can't wait to hear how you've handled this tonight. Right now, though, I'm late for work." She mumbled goodbye to everyone and trudged out the back door to her bookstore, no doubt to pick up some more fancy words to call me later.

"So, Kevin, where am I staying?" Lucille asked, tapping her foot impatiently. "I'd like to get settled so I can start cleaning this house." She reached up and dragged a finger along the top of the doorframe. Who cares if the top of the door is clean? Who even thinks about the top of the door?

"Sarah's room," I announced. Because she's got the cleanest room in our house. And I like annoying my sister. "Sarah can move to the futon in the guest room in the basement."

I think Sarah had something to say, but before she could open her mouth, Lucille was on the move, trotting up to her new room. Seconds later, we saw her dragging the vacuum cleaner from the front closet.

"This might work out okay after all," I whispered to everyone. "Lucille would rather clean than talk, and we *have* kind of let things slide around here lately. She might be so busy with cobwebs and dust bunnies that she forgets to be unpleasant to us."

Sarah scowled at me and made her escape for school, dragging Daniel after her.

Dad shot a blistering glare at Will, who was too

busy picking raisins out of a bagel to notice. Then Will yawned and said, "I didn't catch much sleep last night. Have you noticed that your house makes weird noises?" Dad didn't say a word, just looked toward the door to the basement, where Athena was whimpering. "I'm going to take a little catnap." Will yawned again and headed to my room.

Dad grabbed his briefcase and said to me, "When this is all over, you and I are going to talk about limiting your cell phone access. And email. Texting. Whatever. Forever."

I shrugged. It was obviously going to take a little time for everyone to get on board with the whole togetherness thing. Like olives, face time with extended family is an acquired taste.

I turned my attention to Sparky, Buzz and Brandee, who were the only ones left in the kitchen. They just sat looking at each other. Man, it's always up to Kevin to get the ball rolling.

"So, Buzz," I said, "tell Brandee about yourself. We haven't really had much time to break the ice, get to know each other."

"I'm not sure what to do with my life." Buzz drummed her fingers on the table and looked out the window. If she had just told me that water was no longer wet and Wednesdays were becoming oxygen-optional days, I could not have been more surprised. "Things feel . . . I don't know, blah."

"Well, sure, it's a Monday. Nothing looks good on a Monday. How about this? You skip work today and, um . . ." I paused to think and caught sight of Sparky still hiding under the kitchen table. Poor guy. Even if he did have a scary interest in fire, no one deserved such a wacky intro to their new family. "I've got it! Why don't you and Brandee and Sparky do something?"

"What are you talking about?" Her voice was skeptical, but I could see interest in her eyes.

"You need a change of pace—all you ever do is work these days—and Brandee and Sparky need someone to make them feel welcome to the family. So far, we're not doing such a great job."

"Why they haven't run screaming out the front door, I have no idea," Buzz agreed.

"Which they might do if we leave them here with Lucille."

"She does have that effect on people."

"You could, um, go to a museum or the aquarium or—"

"We could go to the fire station!" Sparky crawled

out from under the table, practically humming with excitement. "My favorite thing."

Wow. Sparky could talk. I hadn't heard him say a word since he got here.

"Really?" Buzz looked doubtful.

"It's fun," Brandee assured her. "You get to see the fire engine and all the equipment and talk to the rescue crew about their jobs."

"Whaddaya say, Buzz?" I used my most cheerful voice. "You up to meeting a few firefighters?"

She perked right up. Buzz would feel comfortable around people with hair-trigger response times; she got her nickname because of how much coffee she drinks and how fast she moves and speaks as a result of all the caffeine.

"You should ask Jack to join you—he seems like the kind of guy who'd like a fire station tour," I told her, thinking he might be a good influence on Sparky at the same time.

"The bummer," Sparky explained to Buzz as they headed out the door with Brandee, "is that the fire engines could go away for an emergency."

"Well, sure, fires happen."

"Don't touch the equipment," Sparky told her.

"Words to live by, kid." The door slammed behind them.

I was dead certain things were going to get crazier around here before they started to calm down, but now I saw that this family get-together had some potential. Finally. I'd have to win everyone over one by one, that much was clear. Lucky for everyone that (a) I'm very persuasive and (b) I'm always up for a challenge.

I couldn't wait to get to school and find a way to tell Tina what I'd done. She'd be touched by my sensitivity.

I'd leave out the part about not intending to invite Will and other family.

And that I hadn't mentioned my emails and texts to Mom and Dad beforehand.

Those kinds of things could easily be misunderstood.

4

The Normal Family Is a Microcosm for All Other Societal Structures

I love school.

Seeing Tina every day makes the research papers, the pop quizzes, the peer pressure and the stress to overachieve worthwhile. I don't know how guys who don't have Tina as their girlfriend handle it all.

My first class, language arts, is bliss, because Tina sits in front of me. Instead of telling her what was going on at my house, I spent forty-seven minutes watching her twist a piece of hair around her finger, which is what she does when she's concentrating. A few strands fell loose and I watched them float down before surreptitiously plucking them off her shoulder. I quickly made an envelope out of lined paper in which to store them. Forever. I have got to get a safe. Something fireproof and waterproof and climate-controlled, wall-mounted, with an unbreakable lock. Treasures like strands of Tina's hair need to be archived and protected the right way.

As I tucked the envelope into my binder, I was thinking that I still needed to come up with something ah-may-zing for us to do on our technically third/officially first mind-blowing, history-making date.

First, I'd come up with the charming and slightly mysterious invitation. Then I had to plan a flawless event. Third, and here's the part most guys don't take into consideration, I'd make sure she had a buttload of stuff to cherish for the rest of her life. I might have to help that along by being sure to save ticket stubs, restaurant menus, rose petals, whatever. You can always tell it's real love if a lot of junk has been saved. Romantic guys like me know this.

I'm not like my best bud, JonPaul, for instance. Just last week, he took his girlfriend, Sam, to the warehouse store with his parents to stock up on detergent, vitamins and mineral supplements, Ace bandages and sterile gauze, gluten-free breakfast cereal and something called spelt, as well as value-sized bottles of facial cleanser, shampoo, body wash and hand sanitizer.

I'm glad JonPaul found someone as understanding of his germaphobic, health-food-obsessed, sports-injury-avoiding life as Sam is. But as a date?

I got so caught up in picturing my perfect date that I didn't hear the bell ring or realize that Tina had left the room—along with everyone else—until I heard Ms. Wisch, my language arts teacher, clearing her throat.

Despite the fact I hadn't yet asked Tina out for the Most Memorable Evening of Her Seemingly Charmed Life, I was feeling happy and hopeful when I headed to social studies. I walked into the room and the first thing I saw were the words AMERICAN POLITICS AS SEEN THROUGH FAMILY UNITY on the board. The project Crosby had told us about on Friday.

"You can see that I have two buckets on my desk." Crosby pointed. "One contains slips of paper on which various relationships have been jotted down, color-coded so you can find your partner. The second bucket contains a number of situations or issues the average family might face over a lifetime. Every student will draw from the first container and establish your family units. Then, together, you'll pull from the second bucket to determine the problem you'll face and solve."

JonPaul drew *grandson* and Jay D. drew *grand-father*. They were so obnoxious about their good luck getting to work together that I wasn't as sad as I probably should have been that they were homeless.

Wheels and Brooke Daniels were cousins with a family member in jail. Dash and Timmy Kurtz were siblings whose mom had a job offer in another state.

Finally, it was my turn; I reached in the bucket and grabbed a slip of paper. I looked down and read it aloud: "Newlywed."

I heard a voice behind me say, "Don't even think of kissing the bride."

I glanced up at Katie Knowles. Correct that: I saw my new wife.

Her slip also said *newlywed*.

Every so often, I have a fleeting sense of hope that Katie and I will maybe be something less than friends but more than adversaries. We have a weird connection; it's like we get each other, but we can't always stand each other. We know what the other person is thinking, but usually I still manage to say the wrong thing. I'm not sure there's a word for what Katie and I are to each other. But *married* is not it.

However . . . Katie is friends with Connie and Connie is friends with Tina, and if I turn out to be an

41

awesome pretend husband, then Katie will tell Connie and Connie will tell Tina and Tina will see me as a family man.

"Hello, wife," I said to her, trying to sound suave and protective in three syllables.

She rolled her eyes and nudged me toward the issue jar. Katie's hand flashed past me and plunged into the bucket. She held two slips of paper when she withdrew her hand.

"Oops, you grabbed two, Katie. Better put one back," I said.

"Are you out of your tiny flipping mind?" She snorted. "This is fate. We were destined to have more problems than the average student."

"Um . . ."

She was peering at me through slitted eyes. "How can you *not* know what this means?"

"Oh, right . . . extra credit."

Katie lives for extra credit the way salmon live to swim upstream, so I knew better than to argue.

"We're trying to pay for a too-expensive house in a downward-trending real-estate market AND one of us has just been laid off from our job."

"Woot woot."

Katie glowed. "This is awesome, Kev. We have so

much to work with here. I just know we're going to get the best grade in the class if we apply ourselves."

"Well, sure." I'm the most apply-yourself kinda guy you'll ever meet. I should have LOVES A CHALLENGE tattooed on my biceps. Maybe RISES TO THE OCCASION on the other arm.

Katie scanned the handouts Mr. Crosby was passing around. "All we need to do this week are these five exercises: summarize our plight, document the challenges we face, assess our individual and joint weaknesses and strengths, visualize our reactions and options and then project the most likely and realistic outcomes."

Was that all? Even though my home had become a bed-and-breakfast for weird relatives, the essence of Kev kicked in. "Don't you think we should also throw together an oral presentation with handouts for the class and a PowerPoint?"

"I like the way you think. Will you have time for all that and be able to get your Fine Arts Fair display ready?"

Fine Arts Fair. That had totally slipped my mind. But I've been to a million museums and I can never tell what half of that stuff is supposed to be. Art is not hard. Everyone knows that. I'd be able to slap something together in no time.

"Why don't you come over after school," I offered. "We can get started on the handouts and organize our time for the rest of the week so we're able to implement our ancillary ideas. When we're done, we can discuss my Fine Arts Fair submission."

Her jaw dropped and then she narrowed her eyes, looking for my angle. I deserved her suspicion; she'd been played before. By me. She must have been able to smell the sincerity oozing out of my pores this time, though, because she finally nodded. "Fine. I have to tutor a couple people right after school, but I'll head to your place when we're done."

"Looking forward to it."

I had plenty of time, energy and great ideas.

I'd ace the social studies project.

And my Fine Arts Fair contribution.

Support Brandee and Will's wedding.

Inspire my family to get along better.

And make sure Tina saw me as her one and only.

Too easy, really.

5

The Normal Family Practices Patience, Tolerance and Creative Problem-Solving Techniques

I bounced into the house after school on Monday, popped my head into the living room and greeted Uncle Will and Brandee, who were reading. They looked like *real* Spencers, sprawled on the couch with books. I didn't ask because I didn't really want to know, but I hoped Brandee and Will hadn't bound Sparky in duct tape to a straight chair in the other room to keep him from trying to burn down the house. Maybe Brandee had ditched Sparky, Jack and Auntie Buzz at the fire station? Either way, Sparky was their problem.

I hollered hello to Lucille, who, from the sounds of it, was cleaning the downstairs bathroom, which always smells like monkey butt.

I petted Athena and Teddy. She was flopped in the entryway, staring at Uncle Will, and Teddy was crouched a few feet away, staring at Athena. "You're a cute couple," I told them. "I think you're going to be very happy together." Athena sighed. Teddy ignored me.

Then I checked the calendar on the fridge for updates. Mom and Dad had two late meetings today—color me shocked; Sarah was with her boyfriend, Doug—ditto; and *Hockey players rule!* meant that Daniel had practice.

I sat down at the kitchen table to do my homework. I started drawing hearts around Tina's name on a sheet of paper and I must have lost track of time, because all of a sudden, I realized that Katie had let herself into the house without knocking and was sitting across the table from me with her textbooks spread out like she belonged here. It was a very peaceful way to start a study session. And the less I say to Katie, the less potential there is for misunderstanding and subsequent apologies.

Katie began outlining our answers to the first question from the assignment packets Mr. Crosby had distributed. I drew a few more hearts.

Lucille swept into the kitchen wearing rubber gloves and a face mask, her hair tied up in a bandana, holding a steaming pail of sudsy water and a mop. I did a double take when I caught sight of JonPaul trailing behind her, clutching a bucket of cleaning supplies and bouncing like Markie does right after I tell him we're going to the park.

"Hey, Kev, Mrs. Spencer just showed me how to clean the hinges on the underside of the toilet seat with Q-tips dipped in bleach." Lucille beamed at him. Finally, she'd found someone as obsessed with cleanliness as she was. Lucille obviously felt more connected to JonPaul than to her own family. Blood may be thicker than water, but detergent trumps both.

JonPaul had been fascinated at lunch when I'd mentioned Lucille was in town and was more excited about cleaning the house than about spending time with the family. He must have sprinted here after school to learn her tricks.

"Is this your little girlfriend?" Lucille asked me.

I knew I'd have to be careful in what I said, because of my weird talent for offending Katie when I don't mean to.

"I'm Katie, Kevin's study buddy," Katie said, sparing me the effort. See? We get each other in ways I can't explain. When we aren't talking, that is. The misunderstandings come when we speak.

47

"I'm Lucille, Kevin's grandmother, and you know JonPaul, I presume?" Katie nodded, but JonPaul was too busy taking notes before the memory of what cleaning magic had transpired in the downstairs bathroom shower stall faded. "I'm here for the wedding this weekend."

"Wedding?" Katie raised her eyebrows at me.

What? Like I had time to tell her about weddings when I'd just found out I was married myself?

"My younger son. He and his bride are"—she dropped her voice to a horrified whisper—*"reading."* Lucille jerked her chin at the living room, her eyes full of amazement that people choose books over scrubbing.

Katie and I got up and peeked around the door. "They're asleep," she said.

"Nooooo!" Lucille wailed.

I distracted her before she could have a meltdown. "Have you gotten the ball rolling?"

"What ball?"

"The wedding ball. You know—caterer, musicians, photographer. Ordering up a justice of the peace. Picking out flowers. Renting tuxedos. Making a guest list and invitations." Am I the only one who watches that show about bridezillas on TV and knows what goes into a wedding?

"Why would I do any of that?"

"I thought mothers were all over wedding planning."

"I am not that kind of mother," she told me. "I'm here to whip this house into shape and get it ready for a wedding."

"Here? Oh, well, um, I kind of thought, I don't know, a restaurant?"

"It would be a shame to have the wedding anywhere else once I've disinfected the toilets and shampooed the carpet and washed the walls and steam-cleaned the—"

I held up a hand. She'd already lost me.

"Well, when you put it that way . . . But you'll tell Mom and Dad the wedding's going to be at the house?"

"If you'll handle everything else."

I hesitated for a second. I'd never planned a wedding before, but I have told Mom and Dad bad news. And I knew which one I'd rather face.

"Deal. How much trouble can a simple family wedding be anyway?"

When Tina and I get married, I'll want to have

a say. For instance, I hope she'll be okay with banana cake and chocolate frosting. I'd drop hints about our future wedding cake on the Date. Planning Will's wedding would help me get ready for my own. Perfect.

Katie opened her mouth like she was about to say something. Then she just smiled and started taking notes again.

Lucille gestured to JonPaul and he followed her into the living room, hanging on her every word. "You won't believe what crumpled-up newspaper and white vinegar will do to that picture window. We'll actually be able to see out of it instead of peering through the layers of smudges."

"Can I come to the wedding?" Katie asked me.

"The more the merrier. Besides, I've got a feeling this will be a can't-be-missed social event."

"You might be right. But we're wasting time when we need to be working on our project."

I sat down at the table and racked my brain. I know there are businesses that exist to plan weddings; what a rip-off. All I had to do was write a list, make some calls and hope for good weather.

Everyone knows a job is as good as half done as soon as you've made the to-do list. I felt super confident once I'd finished it. It was long, sure—that's a lot of stuff when you see it all written down—but again, I was already halfway to finished just getting everything on paper.

I was wondering if we had time to order a cake from the guy on TV who makes them into cool shapes like monsters and trucks, when Sparky wandered in the kitchen and grabbed a bag of chips. Katie looked up from her assignment sheet, saw my new cousin and grabbed my arm.

"Four words, Kev," she whispered, digging her nails in my forearm from excitement. *"Even more extra credit."*

"I'm all about overachieving."

"You're sure?"

"Bring it on. What's a husband for if not to be there for his wife?" I tried to look spouse-y and supportive.

"Great. We're having a baby."

My guts dropped through the soles of my feet.

Katie was taking notes so fast her pencil lead broke. "Anyone can be a young newlywed and worry about paying rent and finding a new job, but we're bound to get A-pluses if we add the crushing responsibility and financial burden of a baby."

"But I don't want a baby."

"You'll change your mind when it's here."

"What do you mean *here*? You're not going to borrow a baby, are you? Remember when I brought Markie to school? Kids and school don't mix."

"Not a real baby. A flour baby. Every teacher at school is obsessed with them—last month, social studies and home ec assigned flour baby projects. But the janitors are furious about the mess of exploded babies. Besides, JonPaul sold me on the benefits of a gluten-free lifestyle. So we're not going to use flour; ours will be a rice sock baby."

"Rice?" I pictured Uncle Will's maggots and gagged. "How about, um . . . popcorn kernels? Then we can pop the baby and eat it when we're done. Maybe watch a movie."

Katie cocked her head, considered, nodded and made a note on her assignment sheet.

"Even if we use popcorn, I'm still not sure this sounds like a good addition to the project," I said. "Remember how I kept losing the flour baby last time?"

"This will give you a chance to redeem yourself. It'll bolster your dismal paternal instincts. And most important of all, a baby'll get me—I mean *us* a ton more bonus points."

Look, I practically invented the idea of extra

credit. But I was just starting to wrap my head around the idea of being married to Katie. Now a kid? Uh-oh.

Katie wasn't done. "We'll add complications: the baby has colic."

"What's colic?"

"Something that makes infants cry inconsolably."

"Let me get this straight: I'm married to you, we're losing our home, I've just been fired and we have a baby who won't stop crying?"

Katie looked incandescent with joy. "Yeah. We're bound to get the highest grade in the whole class."

"I don't want to do this."

"What if you get to name the baby?"

Just what every fourteen-year-old guy dreams of. Oh, what the heck. Katie's not going to give me much leeway; I better have some fun.

"Dumpster Assassin." That's the name I'd picked for myself if I ever became a pro wrestler. Because I think ahead and consider as many options as possible.

Katie looked stunned but said, "Fine. Our baby is Dumpster Assassin."

"And it's a girl."

She pinched her lips together tight. "Of course."

This marriage was off to a better start than I would have ever guessed.

"Just know that I'm going to weigh her regularly to make sure you're not siphoning the kernels out and replacing them with stuffing to make the baby lighter to carry around."

"Of course." Smart as I am, Katie always seems to be one step ahead.

Katie started surfing the Internet, printing a ton of documents. Then she pawed through our pantry and our clean laundry bin.

"We'll encase the popcorn bags in two pairs of tights so the baby doesn't fall apart and leave a trail of innards," she said, cuddling a bag of popcorn kernels.

"Trailing innards are not American Pediatric Association approved." I nodded. "Plus, the baby will have a good tan. A lot of babies are really pasty looking."

She didn't want my help making the baby, so I started filling out the paperwork she'd printed and handed over. Birth certificates, "It's a Girl" announcements, baptismal intentions, immunization schedules, day care applications, college funds, life and health insurance policies, our last will and testament, the declaration of who the guardian would be in case we died.

Man, parenthood is depressing.

"So, look," Katie said, patting the lumpy little doll

she'd made, "do you want to keep her tonight or should I take her home?"

"Does it matter?"

"One of us has to fill out the log book." She waved a small journal in my face. "Keep track of feedings, diaper changings, playtime and brain stimulation, adequate exposure to foreign language tapes and other forms of nontraditional socialization. Did you not get that we are going the extra mile here?"

My eyes started to glaze over and I put up my hands. "Right. Why don't you take Dumpster Assassin home now and then I'll have your, uh, precedent to follow. Later." Technically, never *is* later, so I was telling the truth.

Katie headed home with Dumpster Assassin cradled in her arms and I went downstairs to the family room to chill. I'm at my best when I've had some time to think.

And me at my best was exactly what I needed this week.

So did my family.

A family that now included Katie and Dumpster Assassin.

And Tina, though she didn't know it yet.

6

The Normal Family Is the Link to Our Past and the Guide to Our Future

My grandfather showed up Tuesday morning during breakfast. Correct that: Papa showed up.

Papa's funny, even though he tells awful jokes. He's always doing something cool and he thinks there's not a problem in the world that a good long talk and some ice cream can't fix. He's the best.

Plus, he carries around a wad of ten-dollar bills that could choke a horse. He's always slipping Sarah, Daniel and me ten-spots.

Papa lives in a senior community in Florida and plays a lot of golf and volunteers at the public library and reads to kindergarteners at the elementary school and walks dogs at the animal shelter. Even though he has a busy life pretty far away, we see him a lot. Papa's always sending us plane tickets to come down and hang on the beach with him or else he's banging on our back door at six a.m. to surprise us.

No one batted an eye when he pounded on the kitchen door Tuesday morning.

Besides, I'd texted Papa with the Will and Brandee news. It just took him an extra day and night to drive here from Florida.

Papa brought his girlfriend, Lola, who'd been a Vegas showgirl. A million years ago, but still.

"Papa's got game," Daniel said admiringly when he introduced us to Lola a few years back.

They're a cute couple; Papa wears khakis and golf shirts, and Lola wears short skirts, fishnet stockings and high heels.

The first time we met, she took Sarah, Daniel and me to an arcade, where we blew a fortune on video games. And even though she was in high heels, everyone wanted Lola on their laser tag team.

Lola and Lucille had never seen each other before. In fact, I couldn't remember Lucille and Papa ever being in the same room. They'd gotten divorced before I was born.

"Lucille, you're looking as . . . immaculate as ever,"

Papa said when he spotted her sanitizing the sink. He's so smooth. Even I, with my ability to pick up subtle sarcasm the way dogs hear those ultrasonic whistles, didn't know if his observation was a burn or not.

Lucille looked uncomfortable and started toying with the bottle of tub and tile disinfectant jutting out of her fanny pack. Lola zoomed straight over to Lucille and threw her arms around her boyfriend's ex-wife.

"I feel like I know you, like we're sisters or old friends already." Lola squeezed Lucille and rocked back and forth.

Lucille stiffened but didn't pull away. Eventually, one rubber-gloved hand patted Lola's shoulder a couple times. It was a warmer greeting than the rest of us had ever received from her. Had she ever touched anyone before? I couldn't remember a single instance. Lola didn't notice Lucille's chilliness, and once she broke the hug, she tucked her arm through Lucille's and grinned, clearly believing she'd just made a new BFF.

Good luck with that.

Papa kissed Brandee's cheek and hefted Sparky on his back for a piggyback ride after he lifted Will off the ground in a bear hug. Then he reached into his pocket, pulled out some folded bills and handed them to Daniel and Sarah, who'd been waiting for their turn to throw themselves at Papa.

Mom was chewing her bottom lip. Her thoughts were clear: Why did I ever marry into this nutty family?

Dad just looked numb.

In my self-appointed role of house manager, I said, "Lola and Papa, your call: you can either take the pull-out couch in the basement or the bunk beds in Daniel's room."

"Ooh, bunk beds," Lola said. "It'll remind me of the boarding house off the Strip where I lived when I danced. Except without all the sequins and feathers and half-naked showgirls."

We all took a moment to ponder that mental image.

Finally, I broke the silence. "Then Daniel and I will sleep in the family room."

"C'mon, sweetie," Lola said to Lucille. "Let's take the bride-to-be and go have a spa day. Your cuticles have got to be a hot mess from all that detergent."

Lucille looked terrified, but then, taking a deep breath and voicing the message I'd been telepathically sending her way, she said, "That will be a great chance for us to get to know each other."

Finally! A relative who deserves to call Tina family. Lola was part magic—she made Lucille act like a real person.

"Let's see if Buzz wants to join us," Brandee suggested. "She's a hoot."

No one thought to ask Mom. In their defense, Mom had opened the freezer door and stuck her head in, resting her forehead against a bag of frozen peas. I hoped she didn't think that was the way you meditate.

On their way out the door, Lola squeezed Sparky until his eyes bulged.

"I worked with a dog in Vegas back in the day named Sparky. He could balance on a ball on his two hind legs. We'll have to take you out in the backyard later, see if you can too."

Sparky nodded and high-fived Lola, Lucille and Brandee as they headed out to pick up Buzz.

"Has that poor beast been whining like that since you got here, Will?" Papa peered downstairs.

Papa was the only one of us who hadn't tuned out Athena's yelping. Funny how you can get used to something so awful so fast.

"Not nonstop. But the house is a little tight with so many people, and Athena is sensitive to stress." Will didn't seem to realize he was the reason so many tense folks were under one roof.

"Let's take her for some fresh air, boys," Papa said. Before I knew what was happening, Papa, Will, Sparky and Dad, who looked more alive than he had for a few days, were heading down the street with Athena on a leash.

"I have a headache like you would not believe," Mom told the bag of frozen peas. She pulled her head out of the freezer, glared at me and said, "I'm going to work. I'll see you later. And by later, I might mean never."

Sarah said, "I'm working after school and then going out to a movie with Doug. I'm not planning to come home until everyone in this nuthouse is asleep. For as long as they stay."

Daniel said, "I've got a game tonight, and I'm keeping my fingers crossed that we have overtime. Until next week."

Then all three walked out to the driveway together.

Everyone else was starting to gel as a family unit. Mom and my siblings were the holdouts. Good thing I had a few more days to win them over.

As soon as they were gone, I pulled the wedding

to-do list out of my pocket. Whoa—whole lotta calls. And I only had fourteen minutes before I left for school. I crammed the list back into my pocket. It was Tuesday; plenty of time before the weekend. I'd get started right after school. Maybe even tomorrow. No sense rushing. The assured man takes his time.

Plus, the kitchen, after being so full a few minutes ago, was completely empty, and I couldn't count on that happening again for the rest of the week. So I dug the hazelnut chocolate spread from the back of the pantry where I hide it so no one else will eat it, toasted a couple pieces of bread and sliced a banana. Greatest. Breakfast. Ever.

And total brain food. I jotted a note for Papa and Will to take Sparky over to meet Markie when they got home from their walk. They're about the same age, and Markie only goes to morning preschool. Sparky and Markie. They even sound like they're supposed to be buddies.

And Markie's not interested in flames; he'll be an awesome and age-appropriate good influence on Sparky. Just like I've been on him. Role models for young people are so important. Plus, Sparky could go to preschool with Markie and learn all about colors and numbers and how fire is dangerous and not at all interesting.

Teddy slunk into the room. He looked up at me, narrowed his eyes and gave a baleful meow.

"Athena went for a walk; it's just you and me, buddy."

He swished his tail, hissed and streaked downstairs to await the return of his one true love.

And I headed off to school to see mine.

7

The Normal Family Provides a Safe Environment for Learning to Cope with Disappointment, Frustration and Fear

For the second day in a row, I was even more psyched than I usually am to get to school.

That didn't last long.

I was totally pumped about the one-two punch of family at home and at school, but I wasn't crazy about sharing the chance to be awesome in front of Tina. I was supposed to be the only one to impress Tina with my whole family-guy routine. I could hardly be unique and noteworthy for being a big proponent of family values if the whole class was doing it too. Oh well, I'd find a way.

It was only Day Two of the "American Politics As Seen Through Family Unity" project. But the entire school was obsessed. Just like how the flour baby idea caught fire, APASTFU had infected our school in a cross-curricular frenzy overnight.

Language arts classes were interviewing relatives and then writing papers about their home lives. Art classes were creating family trees in mixed media. All of the math classes were learning about how to budget, invest and pay down debt. The science labs were focused on genetics and heredity. The foreign language labs made posters with family names in different languages: *madre, Mutter, mère, padre, Vater, père* and so on, *y asi sucesivamente, und so weiter, et ainsi de suite*. Luckily, Coach had nothing to add to this curriculum free-for-all and just had us run laps and play badminton.

The highlight of my day is always walking into language arts first period, when I'm astounded by Tina. She has this little freckle on her cheekbone. I can never remember which eye it's under because when I look at her, I forget things like right and left and how to breathe. There's also been some confusion in my mind about whether her middle name is Maria or Marina because I hear music when I think of her and words get muddled. It doesn't matter anyway, because someday Zabinksi will be her middle name.

After she marries me and becomes Katrina Zabinski Spencer.

"Hi, Kevin," she whispered. My ear was in heaven.

I hadn't slept a wink the night before because I had a flashlight under the covers so I could write my script to ask Tina out. I threw in a couple jokes, a few charmingly self-deprecating references to my clumsy past and a compliment about how I think even her earlobes would make Michelangelo weep to know he could never capture such flawless human beauty.

I spent the entire class pretending to take notes, but I was just tweaking my script. Never in history had a guy been so ready to deliver such an irresistible invitation.

I tapped her shoulder the second the bell stopped ringing, and even though I started to forget how to make words when she turned around and smiled at me, I held firm.

But before I could open my mouth, she said, "Katie called last night. She said she'd been working on the social studies project with you and she asked if I wanted to go with her to your uncle's wedding on Sunday. Katie's a sweetie, don't you think?"

All thoughts of my date with Tina flew out of my mind and I concentrated on not exploding at Katie's nosy, take-charge, steal-my-thunder behavior. No matter how hard I try with that girl, we exasperate each other.

And now she'd just robbed me of my big chance. Today should have been epic. But Katie asked Tina out for me before I could do it myself.

And, now, if I asked Tina out on a date, on top of the invite to the wedding, I'd look like some lame and pathetic clinger. Nope, I'd have to wait for another day.

But no one can stay mad while looking at Tina. The United Nations could send her off to strife-ridden war zones across the globe. One flash of her slightly crooked smile and enemies would be shaking hands and helping each other pack up their weapons to go home, after exchanging email addresses and promising to keep in touch.

"I would love for you to come to Uncle Will's wedding," I told her.

She reached out and squeezed my hand—the best RSVP since answering invitations was invented—and I was glad I was still sitting down, because her touch made the room start spinning and I wasn't sure I could keep from falling if I tried to walk. I pretended to be busy organizing my books while she left. As soon as she was gone, although the room looked darker and the oxygen seemed thicker and staler, I was able to stand up.

JonPaul pounced on me as I left class. "Your grandma and I are painting the garage floor this afternoon, Kev. Getting ready for the wedding."

"Who paints garage floors? And why?"

"Mrs. Spencer does. She just texted—she's at the hardware store buying epoxy paint. Easy to clean up, and resists stains."

"Uh-huh." JonPaul never notices my lack of interest in his obsessive rants about cleanliness and germs or nutrition or bodily functions and injuries or his workout routine and sleeping habits.

"After she buys the paint, she'll scrub away oil spots with a degreaser and a stiff-bristle brush."

"You don't say." I kept weaving through the crowded hall.

"I'm so bummed that I don't get to help with the pressure washer."

"Who wouldn't be?" We were at my locker, and I shoved my language arts folder in and pulled out my social studies book.

"But she promised that I'll be able to help apply primer using a roller on an extension pole after school."

"You're living the dream, buddy." JonPaul may well

be immune to sarcasm. It's kind of a waste for me to be his friend when he doesn't appreciate my humor.

"The primer needs at least eight hours to dry." Jon-Paul sounded as worried as when he found out about the inefficacy of the topical application of vitamin E oil in reducing or removing scars after he messed up his knees tripping over a hurdle during track.

Even when I don't care, I still care. "Text Lucille and tell her to rent an industrial-strength fan while she's at the hardware store. That'll speed up the drying process."

"That's awesome, Kev, thanks. Because we're also supposed to wait at least twenty-four hours before applying the second coat of paint. And the wedding this weekend doesn't give us much wiggle room in case it rains."

"While you're in the garage anyway, can you ask Lucille to fix the door opener?"

He sent a quick text to Lucille.

Then we went to social studies, where everyone huddled with their partners. I nodded and *uh-huh*ed my way through Katie's long recitation of Dumpster Assassin's first night at home. She had tapped into a webchat for new mothers in Hawaii ("The timing was perfect, Kev!") to collect firsthand data. Katie stayed up all night, for authenticity in terms of the new-parent fatigue, and multitasked by processing applications for the Fine Arts Fair while pacing back and forth patting Dumpster Assassin's back.

"So I'll give you the baby after the last bell, okay?" she said as she left class.

I'm not psychic, but I could tell that Dumpster Assassin was going to make a miraculous recovery in my care and sleep through the night. I'd share that good news with Katie tomorrow.

I was grateful she was willing to wait until after school to hand off the baby; I couldn't imagine how embarrassed I'd feel if she made me take it at school. Whew!

When I walked into the cafeteria for lunch, I felt like I'd teleported into another dimension. Normally, everyone sits in the same place and with the same people. Very reliable. Today, however, people had gathered in unusual clusters; the entire social order of the school was in disarray. Although I'd seen how my social studies class had been partnered up, I was taken aback to see some of the pairings from the other classes.

Connie Shaw, who normally sits two tables over

and on Tina's right because they're BFFs, was at my table. Practically on Cash Devine's lap. She'd fallen pretty hard for him recently. Cash looks like the kind of guy a girl who looks like Tina should date, and Connie . . . well, as I've heard Mom say about people who aren't winning any beauty contests, Connie's the kind of girl who will grow into her looks.

Before I could decide if the guy-code thing to do would be to help Cash escape (even though part of me thought leaving him to fend off Connie on his own was nothing more than he deserved for being such a curve-wrecker in the looks department), I was stopped dead by a vicious yank from behind.

Katie wheeled me around and slammed Dumpster Assassin into my arms. "That sneaky Milania Zeman is trying to rename the Fine Arts Fair the Athletic Association Fine Arts Fair. As if the student government isn't just as involved and supportive of the arts! I have to put a stop to this right away. I called an emergency intervention with the principal. Obviously, a meeting like that is no place for a baby."

"Oh, I don't know. Uncontrolled rage gets a bad rap. . . ."

She dashed off for the principal's office before I

could explain why I believe babies are never too young to learn that it's important to manage your temper. And before I could refuse to take the baby. I tried to shove Dumpster Assassin into my backpack before anyone noticed, but my lunch buddies Wheels, Dash, Jay M., Jay D., Scott, Greggie, Todd and Kurt had seen the whole thing.

There was nothing to do but saunter over to their table, looking as if I didn't have a care in the world except for rewriting the Rules of Swagger to include carrying dolls. I hoped Tina saw the way I radiated self-confidence and paternal care.

Nope. She was sitting at another table, deep in conversation with Sean Sexton.

After Cash Devine, Sean Sexton was the best-looking eighth-grade guy. When I first got interested in Tina, I'd ranked all the guys in my class to assess my competition. Sean, in a pre-Cash world, had beaten out JonPaul for the most handsome. I had to deduct points from JonPaul for his germ and health obsessions. For every weird habit you have, you lose a degree of hotness.

Dang. Tina and Sean got paired up on the project. Okay, keep calm, do not panic, don't act like you used to. She's your girlfriend, you have a date set up for this weekend, a wedding date, this is just homework. Don't act crazy.

It's not crazy to squeeze yourself between two people who are working when there's really no space for you and no logical reason to be there and you happen to be holding a doll.

It's super crazy.

"Hey, Tina. Hi, Sean!" A big cheery smile and a friendly tone takes the nutty edge off any gesture. I hoped Tina and Sean knew that rule too.

Luckily, the fire-drill bell rang.

Tina and I got separated in the stampede out of the building. Which bummed me out until Katie came flying up, screeching about Dumpster Assassin. I was glad Tina was nowhere near as I tried to comfort a sobbing Katie.

"Don't cry, Katie. Everything's fine. The, uh, baby's safe. Here"—I thrust the journal and a pen in her hand—"why don't you log this event? Ensuring the safety of your child."

Katie wiped her face and started writing. "Good thinking. I almost lost it there, didn't I?"

Who wouldn't burst into tears at the thought of a bag of popcorn kernels being left unattended in the lunchroom during a fire drill? I didn't say that, though, because she was calm again. I didn't even mind that she ordered me to keep bouncing and rocking our colicky baby until we could go back to class.

Katie didn't see me cram Dumpster Assassin in my locker as I grabbed my Spanish book. I've spent a lot of time observing my folks, so I know that good coparenting operates on a need-to-know basis.

And Katie didn't need to know I was starting to get overwhelmed by my family. Both of my families.

8

The Normal Family Supports, Guides and Understands the Various Maturity Levels of Every Member

Tuesday afternoon I bounced home, eager to see Papa and hoping he'd be in the mood for a little midafternoon snack. When Papa's in town, we go to Ruby's Shake Shack for hand-churned French vanilla ice cream with homemade hot fudge sauce, sliced bananas, slivered almonds and a tower of fluffy whipped cream.

And I knew that some ice cream, maybe a ten-spot slipped in my pocket and a good talk with Papa would calm me down.

Papa's usually waiting on the front step for me when I get home after school. Tuesday, however, some hippy-dippy bald guy wearing combat boots, baggy fatigue pants and a peace sign T-shirt was sitting on the top step, playing the guitar. Lola sat next to him, softly patting a set of bongo drums.

"Kevin! Honey! This is my grandson, Brad."

Brad, still strumming, nodded at me and spelled, "*S-N-O-W-P-H-I-S-H.*"

"Excuse me?"

"My old name was Brad. My new name is Snow-phish. Snowphish Om."

"Really."

Lola smiled and shrugged.

"Yeah." Snowphish started twisting the pegs on his guitar and plucking the strings. I'm not musical, but even I could tell he was doing the opposite of tuning his instrument, because the fillings in my molars started to vibrate from the sound. "My chosen nomenclature is more aligned with where I am artistically, you know?"

"No, not at all."

"Few do. It's a learned process. Daring. Not many take the risk to open themselves in search of the purpose and meaning of the universe and then seek the name meant for them rather than blindly taking what was randomly assigned."

"I've always been good with Kevin."

"Kevin. Keeeeeeeeeevin. Kevvvvvvvvvvvvin. Kev-innnnnnnnnnn." Snowphish tried out my name in several different ways to get a feel for it, I guess. "Yeah, you know, I dig that. It's very wah."

"Wah?"

"Yeah. Wah is the cosmic flow and universal energy that pervades and fuels every living cell. Wah is very peaceful and yet inspiring. Wah makes you want to take a nap and then save the world."

"Uh . . . huh." I like Lola, and she was sitting right there listening to us, so I tried to be polite and stop myself from asking how many concussions he'd suffered. One of the guys on Daniel's hockey team sounded like this after he'd been checked into the boards super hard during regionals last year.

"Hi, Dutchdeefuddy." That's my name according to Markie. At least in his mind, it means best, most favorite buddy in the world forever. Markie stood beside me, beaming.

I hadn't noticed Markie's mother dropping Sparky and him off in the driveway after preschool and then zooming away so I could babysit.

Sparky took one look at Snowphish and hurried to hide behind Lola. Markie stood in front of Snowphish, staring at his shiny scalp.

77

"Where's your hair?"

"Hair is death," Snowphish told Markie, nodding solemnly.

Markie looked horrified, gently patting the top of his head.

"Hair is nothing more than dead cells. Bad energy, little guy. Blocks the flow of wisdom free-floating in the atmosphere from permeating your head. Hair is a buffer between you and the truth. Hair keeps you ignorant and downtrodden. Hair is an oppressive regime."

Before Markie could get to a pair of scissors, I told him, "Don't even think about it. He's talking about *for him*. It has nothing to do with you and your hair. Or intelligence. Or, um, human rights."

Markie looked disappointed that I wouldn't let him chop off all his hair. I moved fast to lift his spirits. "Here." I pulled Dumpster Assassin out of my bag and handed her to him. "We're pretending that's a real baby and you can be the babysitter today."

"How much are you paying me?"

"Three dollars."

He held out his hand. I placed three dimes on his grubby little paw. Markie's sharp about some things, but he doesn't have the faintest idea about money.

Sparky emerged from his hiding spot behind Lola and sat next to Markie as they studied Dumpster Assassin.

Clearly, a day together at Markie's preschool had really cemented their friendship. Just like I planned.

"Where's Papa?" I asked Lola.

"He's with Lucy, disinfecting the caulk in the bathroom tubs with toothbrushes and a paste made of baking soda and hydrogen peroxide."

Lucy. Huh. I didn't see the nickname fitting her, but okay. "How'd you get out of cleaning?" I asked Lola.

"I didn't. Lucy had me degreasing the kitchen cabinets."

"I didn't know our kitchen cabinets were greasy."

"Neither did I. Luckily, Brad—I mean Snowphish called and I had to dash to get him. I should go back inside and offer to help." But Lola picked up the bongos again and rat-a-tat-tatted along with Snowphish's strumming.

I glanced over at Markie and Sparky. They were sitting on Dumpster Assassin. I'd recently read a book to Markie about how mother birds sit on their eggs, so I knew they meant well. Plus, they were very quiet. I encourage quiet playtime for the children in my care. And Sparky looked—if it was at all possible—like the urge to investigate what causes fires had died down. Or maybe that was my own wishful thinking.

I looked back at Snowphish. I should have figured someone else would show up. "So, how long are you visiting? And, um, why?" Lola had never mentioned a grandson.

"The spirits spoke to me and guided me here."

Lola speaks Snowphish and translated for me: "He ran out of money two towns over. It was a total coincidence I was so close. Instead of wiring him a few bucks like I usually do, I picked him up, and now we get to spend a couple days together."

"What were you doing two towns over?" I asked.

"I'm on a vision quest," he said. "Allowing my sacred and all-wise id, rather than my infected and material-bound ego, to direct my journey and determine my path."

"He's hitching rides, singing on street corners and in crummy dives for spare change." Lola winked. No wonder Papa's crazy about her.

Lola and I listened to Snowphish strum. "He really makes you appreciate the phrase 'a sour note,' doesn't he?" Lola asked. We both knew it was better than going inside and being told to clean the oven. Markie turned Dumpster Assassin's diapers into turbans for him and

80

Sparky. Katie would have had a fit, but I thought it was a good look. Besides, she'd sent an overnight bag with other clothes. I tossed it to Markie, and he and Sparky dressed her in every single piece of clothing. Dumpster Assassin looked very plump by the time Mom and Dad yelled "Dinner!"

Dad had brought home a few bowls of salad and Mom slammed five boxes of pizza on the counter. Everyone loaded a plate and then disappeared.

Markie dragged Sparky and Dumpster Assassin under the table with a plate of pizza. Making a hide-out is the sign of a perfect friendship. They reminded me of a mini-me and a little JonPaul.

I was the only one sitting at the table when Katie called. "Put Dumpster on the line."

"Dumpster *Assassin*, and what do you mean, put her on the line?"

"Look, if we have to be apart, I want to keep in contact. I'm logging each phone call as proof of my commitment. You should make sure you're document- ing each diaper change and feeding, and listing all the songs you sing and foreign language tapes you play and picture books you read. No, wait, picture books might not be enough of a challenge; read Plato and Aristotle instead."

"Nothing but the best," I agreed, while holding the phone to the popcorn-kernel doll Markie and Sparky had put to bed in the broiler drawer of the oven under a dish towel. Have at it, Katie.

Markie and Sparky fed Athena their pizza crusts and I picked the sausage off my slice to share with Teddy. The boys ran into the living room as soon as Athena threw up, and I was left to clean up after her. Barf really bonds people, even if one of them is a dog. After I was done spritzing the floor with Lucille's special disinfectant, I sat down with Athena's head in my lap, pulled out the wedding to-do list and started making calls.

Wow. Weddings are expensive. I'd only called three of the names on my list and the prices they were mentioning made me a little sick. Or else it was Athena's breath.

"There's got to be a better way to throw a wedding together," I told Athena, who yawned.

Sarah stormed in the back door, took one look at Snowphish Om, who was washing his socks in the kitchen sink, and said, "I'll be at Buzz's if you need me." She flounced out to Buzz's apartment above the garage.

Sarah's been looking for an excuse to move out for

years. And besides, maybe having horrible Sarah live with Buzz for a while would give her a new appreciation for how good her life was.

"Snowphish, you're sleeping in the guest room in the basement tonight. I hope you like futons."

"Subterranean space. Allows me to catch the vibrations of the earth in my core."

"That was my thinking."

Markie's mother rang the doorbell to pick him up. Before he left, Markie gave me a bone-crushing hug.

"What's that for?" I asked.

"For giving me Sparky."

"You like him?"

"Yeah."

"What's so great about him?"

"He belongs to me."

"I didn't REALLY give him to you. You know that, right?" I was a little worried that Markie might think Sparky was like the baseball cap I'd bought for him last week—a keeper.

Markie looked at me like I'd suddenly lost a billion brain cells. "He was my line buddy at school."

"Your what?" I'd forgotten my preschool lingo.

"Someone to make sure you don't get lost going to the bathroom."

"That a big problem at your school?"

"Not for me. Nicky Abbinante wanders, though. But Sparky is my forever line buddy. Everyone needs them."

Markie always teaches me stuff I don't know I need to learn. I wasn't sure what he'd just taught me, but I'd figure it out.

Katie called two more times before I went to bed, burning up all my minutes and annoying the living daylights out of me until I suggested video chatting. I aimed the laptop camera at Dumpster Assassin and went to sleep.

But even *that* wasn't good enough. Katie called me in the middle of the night to remind me to make sure the baby was still breathing. I'm a rational, fun-loving guy, but I hadn't slept for the past two nights.

"It's a onesie filled with popcorn," I snarled at Katie at 3:17 a.m. "What do you mean IS SHE STILL BREATHING?"

"Parental tension is bad for the baby. Use your calm voice, please. If this were a real baby—"

I cut her off. "If Dumpster Assassin were a real baby, is what you meant." Katie's not the only one who can be nitpicky in the middle of the night.

"Right. If . . . Dumpster Assassin were a real baby,

we'd be checking on it, I mean her, several times during the night. For feedings and making sure she wasn't getting stuck in her bedding and that the temperature and air quality were sufficient."

Right. I sighed and made a notation in the log book.

Then I turned off my phone and unplugged my laptop so she couldn't check in on us again.

Even so, I didn't catch a wink the rest of the night. Snowphish Om chants in his sleep.

This was the third night of the Kevin Spencer Sleep Deprivation Project, and I was starting to understand why keeping someone awake is considered a form of torture.

9

The Normal Family Values Each Other's Opinions, Finding Solutions in Collective Feedback

Because I hadn't slept Tuesday night, I snuck out of the house Wednesday morning before anyone woke up. Or any new folks arrived.

I made a beeline for the doughnut store on my way to school and slurped down a mega coffee with ten sugar packets and three double-chocolate doughnuts. This sugar-and-caffeine supercharge carried my exhausted butt along, but I was so wiped out that the day was a lot of blurry faces and nonsensical conversations. My hands were shaking and my heart was pounding in a way that couldn't have been good. Even Tina was just a sparkly blob in my peripheral vision.

I staggered home from school hoping for a nap.

Katie had Dumpster Assassin for the night, so I was free to snooze.

When I got home, Mom was sitting at the kitchen table and Buzz was lying flat on her back in the middle of the floor.

"So, what's new?" I asked cautiously as I stepped over Buzz.

"Auntie Buzz is being poisoned by her apartment," Mom told me. "Apparently, the epoxy paint Mrs. Spencer and JonPaul used in the garage made her apartment uninhabitable."

"Well, sure, it's about time we made room for more family." I sat down next to Mom and we rested our heads on our crossed arms on the table.

"Where are you thinking of putting her?" Mom asked me. "And Sarah, since she moved in with Buzz, geez, was it only yesterday?"

"Feels like an eternity, doesn't it?"

"Pretty much."

"Looks like she's already decided she's going to sleep there." I pointed at Buzz.

"Don't be ridiculous," Buzz said without opening her eyes. "I'm going to sleep on the living room couch. Good thing Sarah broke the curio cabinet, because now there's room for her to set up an air mattress in that corner."

"Isn't there a limit on the number of people who can sleep under one roof?" I asked Mom.

"I wish."

I heard Athena's nails clicking on the floor and raised my head from my arms. She and Teddy curled up next to Buzz on the floor. Buzz looked less lonely.

Lonely. Maybe Buzz's recent bad mood had been not a funk but loneliness. She lives by herself. Above a garage. How sad is that?

"I have a great idea!" I said. Because inspiration and amazing plans are my best friends.

"Excellent," Mom told the place mat. "The one thing this family needs is another good idea."

"Buzz should marry Jack!" Yes, I had marriage on the brain. But what a stroke of brilliance: Buzz's housing problem solved; plus, she's been a lot less Buzzy since dating Jack. And he's great. He really rolled with the whole scene when Uncle Will showed up the other evening.

"Jack does have a calming effect on me," Buzz mused. "And he already asked me to marry him. We got a license, but then I chickened out."

"He doesn't seem like the kind of guy to take back an offer just because you shot him down," I told her.

"Married? Again? Already?" Mom started waving

her hands in front of her face like the room had suddenly gotten really warm.

"Probably." Buzz rested her forearm across her eyes.

Man. When Tina breaks the news to her family that I've proposed, she's gonna be a lot more excited than Buzz.

"I think I'm really on to something," I told Mom. "Give it a little time to settle in." It takes other people a while to come to terms with what I grasp immediately.

"But you've only known him for a few weeks." Mom put her forehead on the table again.

"She's *known* him for years—he works at her bank," I pointed out. "Though, yes, she's only been *dating* him for a few weeks."

Auntie Buzz didn't seem as jazzed as your typical bride-to-be. Come to think of it, Will and Brandee had been pretty laid-back about the whole thing. Luckily, I've got enough wedding fever for the whole family.

Everyone turned up in the kitchen at once. Uncle Will came in from the living room with Brandee and Sparky. Papa and Lola trailed behind them. Lucille and JonPaul trooped in from the garage, removing their face masks. Snowphish Om appeared, strumming his guitar.

"What's new?" Will asked.

"Buzz is engaged," I announced.

"Great timing, Buzz. The gang's all here," Lola said.

Not the whole gang; I whipped out my phone and texted Dad, Daniel and Sarah.

Then I fired off a quick text to Jack, congratulating him and letting him know the Spencers had decided it was okay for him to marry Buzz. Time and location to come.

"I love your weddings, Buzzy," Papa said. "Shame I had to miss that phony ceremony in Mexico. Have you set the date?"

"No. I just decided thirty seconds ago." Buzz hadn't risen from the floor, but at least she'd opened her eyes to look at the people hovering over her.

"You could do a double ceremony with Uncle Will and Brandee," I suggested. "This weekend."

"No sense waiting, I guess." Buzz squinted at the ceiling, considering.

"The more the merrier," said Brandee, nodding.

"We wanted a family wedding," Will said. "And you can't get much more family than sharing your wedding day with your brother's sister-in-law."

"It really does tie us all together," I agreed.

"I could compose a song for the ceremony," Snow-phish said. "I think the institution of marriage is a threat to individual liberty and gender equality, and I question the necessity of having relationships sanctioned by religious authorities. But I'm feeling very artistically motivated. Good energy."

I yanked my to-do list out of my pocket and crossed off *music*.

"We're going to need to shop for dresses," Lola said. "It might be tricky to find something special at the last minute. But when I worked at the casino we used to say there's no dress so ugly it can't be fixed with enough sequins and rhinestones. I once went onstage hot-glued into my costume because the zipper broke."

I crossed *wedding dress* off my list too. Way to pull it together! Spencers, you are worthy of being related to me.

"Buzz should wait. Not rush into anything," Mom said. Everyone pretended not to hear.

"What about the men? What should we wear?" Papa asked.

"Tuxedoes are too formal," Uncle Will said. "Michael has a million business suits and they're all dark. We can each borrow one; he won't mind."

I'd been updating Dad, Sarah and Daniel with play-by-play texts since the conversation started. Now I told Dad we were raiding his closet for clothes and that he should swing by the hardware store to buy an air mattress for Sarah on his way home.

Papa, Sparky and Will took Athena for a walk. Snowphish Om went to the basement to compose. Lucille and JonPaul headed back to the garage to see if the toxic stench of the epoxy paint was dissipating.

Brandee had fallen asleep in her chair and Buzz was now out cold in the middle of the kitchen floor. I think Mom might have dozed off too, because her head was buried in her arms again and she'd stopped objecting.

I was studying my list. "Call the baker, order two cakes," I muttered.

"Papa told me you had a baking business, Kev," Lola said as she scrolled through pictures of wedding dresses on her tablet.

"Yeah, that was a while back, but hey! Shut. The. Front. Door. I can make the cake!" Lola beamed at me while I checked off *cake*. I don't know why I hadn't thought of that immediately—Sam, JonPaul and I had churned out hundreds of baked treats a night when we were in business, and a cake couldn't be any harder than cookies and bars. I'd take off from my Saturday jobs at the waste company and the storage facility and knock out a couple of cakes. JonPaul would be around; I'd make sure Sam was free, and we'd be good.

I went downstairs to do a computer search of banana cake recipes. Might as well use this as a dry run for my own wedding cake. I'd just hand Tina a plate and watch her realize that I am funny, thoughtful, romantic, family-minded *and* a mind-blowing baker.

There was no way Tina could fail to appreciate ole Kev. Look how things work out for me: My initial plan had merely been to get Will and Dad in touch again. But I'd wound up bringing the entire family together under one roof, was organizing a double wedding and had solved Buzz's life problems. On top of helping Katie destroy any potential academic competition as her partner for the APASTFU project. While I was setting Tina up for a glimpse of her future as part of my family.

And doing it all virtually sleep-free.

Whew. No one I'm related to could handle the pressure and responsibilities. It's hard to be me; good thing I'm doing it and not anyone else.

10

The Normal Family Unites in a Crisis, Growing Stronger from the Shared Experience

Thursday morning, I took a thermos of hot chocolate made with coffee to drink between classes. No sleep for the fourth night. Snowphish Om had discovered that the dead of night was the most inspirational time to compose, and having thirteen people in one house meant that someone was flushing the toilet all night long.

Another surreal morning of meaningless sound and blobs of color that were people moving past me. Luckily, I've mastered the art of looking interested in class when I'm zoning out. I don't think anyone noticed I wasn't checked in.

As we left social studies, Katie handed off

94

Dumpster Assassin to my custody. Correct that: she *tried* to hand off DA, but then I turned in the doorway, thinking I'd left my lucky pen on my desk, and slammed the baby carrier into the doorframe with a sickening *thwack*. Katie yelped, grabbed the doll and fled down the hall.

By the time lunch rolled around, thanks to some hefty gulps of chocolaty java, I was feeling pretty perky. I was awake and alert, and the ringing in my ears had died down. Maybe I was learning to live without sleep.

Life was good.

For me, at least.

JonPaul, on the other hand, wasn't himself when I got to the cafeteria. He was eating potato chips and French fries. Deep-fried food. And simple carbs. At the same time. On a weekday.

JonPaul only eats junk on Saturdays. And there wasn't a radish or a wheatberry or a ginger-apple-kale smoothie in sight to balance the toxin dump. He sneezed right in his hand and didn't run off to lather, rinse, repeat or squeeze hand sanitizer in his palm. He just wiped his hand on his jeans and tipped candy-coated chocolates into his mouth straight from the bag.

"What's up, buddy?" I asked, watching him raid my lunch sack for cookies.

"Sam wants to break up with me."

I was so surprised that I barely noticed he spewed gingersnap crumbs in my face.

"Shut. Up." They'd only been going out a little while, and of course, we're only fourteen, but I had visions of JonPaul and Sam and Tina and me happily double-dating for life.

"Yeah, she thinks I'm either spending too much time with Mrs. Spencer or at the gym." JonPaul didn't bother to wipe the chocolate milk mustache off his upper lip after taking a long gulp. I snuck a glance at the label; it wasn't even low-fat. JonPaul, buddy, what's happening to you? "She said I care more about cleaning and my health than I do about her."

"And that bothers her?"

"Crazy, right?"

"Yeah, women: they're hard to figure."

"Uh-huh." JonPaul burped and eyed Jay M.'s hamburger. I grabbed him by the arm and tried to pull him out of the cafeteria behind me. It was like tugging an airplane. Chips and fries and candy and cookies and fatty milk were one—okay, five things—but cafeteria mystery meat?

Besides, I'd glanced over and seen Sean Sexton sitting next to Tina. Oh, sure, they had papers spread out in front of them to work on the APASTFU, but I wouldn't be able to eat knowing he was sitting close enough to see the way the baby hairs at her temples catch the light when she tips her head.

Dating a girl like Tina meant I worked hard to not become insanely jealous. I don't know how super-models' boyfriends handle the pressure; maybe there's an online support group for guys who date beautiful girls. If there's not, I should start one.

"C'mon, buddy," I said, trying to lead JonPaul out of the cafeteria. "Let's get some air, clear our heads."

Normally, when he's bummed, JonPaul will hit the gym, run a few laps. I was going to suggest that, but then I remembered that he's always talking about how incomplete carbohydrate metabolism results in the formation of toxic metabolites such as pyruvic acid, which accumulates in the brain and nervous system, interfering with the respiration of the cells.

Huh. I *do* listen to JonPaul. Well, I don't listen, but I retain information. Strenuous physical activity could have killed him just then.

So I led him to where I go when I'm upset: the library. Sitting and reading never hurt anyone.

Katie was already there, of course. So was Dump-ster Assassin. Of course. Katie was working on

APASTFU, of course. The three—correct that, *four* of us grabbed a study room, and after taking a closer look at JonPaul and glancing at me for that kind of wordless explanation we've recently mastered, Katie typed and clicked on her laptop before sliding it over to JonPaul. I glanced over his shoulder and saw him writing down the recipe for a restorative juice cleanse regimen.

Whew! JonPaul was back.

I grabbed his phone and composed a text to his girlfriend: *Sam—hope2CU l8er. I made special plans 4 the weekend.* I added a smiley face and a heart for good measure and pressed Send. JonPaul was going to need to step up his game to hold on to her. I was just helping.

Katie handed me a few paragraphs to proofread. I found a single typo that I hated to point out since I've never seen Katie make a mistake before and I wasn't sure that I was up for her reaction. But she took it well—a small squeak of dismay and then her fingers were flying across the keyboard to correct the misspelling.

JonPaul was looking at his phone and grinning. Sam had replied.

Tomorrow was the last day of APASTFU, but Katie and I nailed down the final part of the assignment a day early.

"Here." Katie handed me a notebook to initial. "The Dumpster Assassin physical care and mental stimulation log."

"Oh, I see you added photos of her being read to, watching educational programming and interacting with Athena and Teddy so she'd develop empathy for dependent creatures."

"Visual aids get extra credit. Now help me scan everything from the color copier to a flash drive and then we'll email Crosby our project."

"And thus concludes our starter marriage," I said a little while later as we pushed the Send button together.

We. Are. Awesome.

"So," Katie said as we left the library, "how's everything at your house?"

How do you summarize a week like the one I was having chez Spencer? Not even I could find the right words.

She patted my shoulder. "Hang in there. Just a couple more days."

Just a couple more days . . . Oops—I might not have managed my time as well as I could have. I felt the list in my pocket. I still had a ginormous amount to pull together. But then I remembered: I thrive under pressure. Whew! Close one; I almost panicked. Not Kevinlike.

"Have you finished working on your Fine Arts Fair submission?" she asked.

Then I did panic. I KNEW I should have written that on my list.

"I may have. This week has been such a blur, I may have done it and forgotten." When all else fails, hope for the best.

"I've read about artists who are at their most productive in a fog of sleep deprivation," she said, nodding.

If that had happened to me this week, it would be so cool.

Katie peeled off and I kept walking, chewing my lip.

Did Jack get my text? Did Buzz bring him up to speed on the wedding? Because I could teach classes in efficiency, I texted, *u kno ur getting married this weekend rite? Pls confirm.*

I wished Lucille was interested in something other than cleaning, because her energy level would be super helpful.

I smoothed the list on my thigh and jotted *clean the house.* Then I crossed it off. I love the relief of completing a task.

Apparently, Papa and Uncle Will thought taking

Athena for long walks was a valuable prenuptial contribution, because that was all they'd done.

Brandee had been really sweet about Buzz's stealing her spotlight by sharing her wedding day, and I guess that was all I could ask for. She was, after all, taking responsibility for Uncle Will.

Sparky hadn't started a single fire all week. Great team spirit, buddy. Plus, he was bringing home wild finger paintings from Markie's preschool and had learned to count to five in French.

I was sure Snowphish Om's song was going to be awful, but he was contributing what he could.

Lola was excited about the dresses. Too bad she couldn't get as stoked about renting chairs and making a guest list.

Guests. Hmm. This was one task I might have let go too long. I couldn't even be sure the people who lived in my house would show up. Mom and Dad were spending more time at work than usual, which is really saying a lot. Sarah and Daniel showed up each night moments before curfew and went straight to bed.

I blitzed everyone in my address book with an invite. I'd swipe Mom's and Dad's and Buzz's phones when I got home and access their contacts too. I made a big X through *guest list* on my list.

Then I took a picture of my list with my phone and texted it to everyone: *pick 1 thing u can do 4 the wedding. Then do it asap. leave note on fridge what u picked. Thx—Kev.*

Delegating. People love it. Should have thought of it sooner.

I hoped someone was preparing a toast in my honor Sunday.

To be safe, I put it on my list: *write toast.*

I still had to slap together something to submit to the Fine Arts Fair and make sure JonPaul started putting Sam first so she wouldn't dump him. Because Tina might not like her boyfriend's best friend hanging around like a third wheel.

I wrote those things on my list. Then I was suddenly sick to death of the list.

But I was keeping my fingers crossed that sometime in the past day or two, I'd experienced that artistic state that might have caused me to be secretly productive.

People used to think the four-minute mile was impossible too.

And if anyone was going to surprise themselves with a job well done, it was going to be me.

11

The Normal Family Does Not Limit Itself to the Sharing of Genes or Legally Binding Constructs

When I got home from school Thursday, I was hoping I'd see Papa waiting for me on the front step. That today would be the day we'd finally slip away for hand-churned French vanilla ice cream with homemade hot fudge sauce, sliced bananas, slivered almonds and a tower of fluffy whipped cream.

Instead, I found a glum-looking Goober sitting in front of my house, his head in his hands. Goob is JonPaul's cousin; he's in college. Kind of. Markie and Sparky were next to him, mimicking his pose. I'd have to tell Markie's mom that Goober was not a reliable person to leave Markie with when she dropped him off.

I pulled Dumpster Assassin out of my backpack

and, now that she'd served her purpose, gave her to Markie and Sparky. Markie opened his koala backpack and pulled out a bunch of his old baby clothes—Markie's always prepared—and started dressing her.

"You look bummed," I said, and sat next to Goober. "What's up, Goob?"

"Love, man."

"How is Betsy?" Goober had recently started dating one of my neighbors who was away at college. I couldn't figure out what she saw in him; Betsy's one of the coolest, smartest, sweetest girls I know, while Goober is a lot like Pointillism—you don't want to look too long or get too close because then you'll get nauseated and need to back away quick.

"She's too far away." Goober sounded a lot like Teddy when he pines for Athena. I know Teddy's a cat and Goober's a . . . whatever, but they shared the same mournful, lonely, aching tone. "She's coming home this weekend for a visit, though, and that's when I'm going to ask her to transfer to my school and move back home."

I shook my head hard like a cartoon dog. Betsy goes to a top university that has waiting lists; Goober goes to a school that ranks high on party school lists. "Why?"

"I miss Bets. All the time. My life is agony without her."

"But you've only known her ..." I counted the weeks since I'd first introduced them.

"I wouldn't have expected such negativity from my own flesh and blood, dude."

"Not us. You and *JonPaul* are cousins."

"Yeah, but you and JonPaul are brothers, and *that*"—Goober looked proud of his deductive reasoning—"makes *us* cousins!"

What kind of standards did Goober's college have for accepting students? I used to think Goober was playing up the dumb bunny routine as a gimmick. The more time I spent with him, the more he shot down that theory. Markie rolled his eyes at me and pointed his finger at his head, twirling it in circles. Loco. Even Sparky giggled under his diaper turban.

"Okay, right, sure, cousins." I winked at Markie and Sparky. "But how do you expect me to support this crazy idea?"

"You don't have to be supportive. Just help me figure out what to say to her, and how to get our folks on my side, and then be there for me, and point out to her that one school is as good as any other, but a love like ours is one in a million."

"Sure, just as long as you're not asking for support."

"It's not like I'm needy and helpless and haven't got a clue."

I was trying to find the words to Strongly Encourage Goober to Rethink His Plan when he cocked his head and sat up. "Is that bongos? Do I hear bongos?" Betsy was forgotten.

If you can't reason with someone, distract them. Markie taught me that.

"Yeah, it's Snowphish Om."

"You never told me Snowphish played the bongos."

I'd never told him about Snowphish *at all*. I should be getting used to the things Goober fixes on during a conversation. "It's a new development."

Goober jumped up and blew into my house like he lived there.

I was going to follow him in; that was the right thing to do. Introduce him to everyone, maybe call Mom and see if I could do anything to help get dinner ready, definitely make a few more calls to photographers and caterers and find someone to perform the ceremony and . . .

But a quick glance inside changed my mind.

Lucille was on a ladder in the living room dismantling the ceiling fan. Snowphish and Goober were sitting on the love seat, jamming. Lola was wrapping Auntie Buzz and Brandee in some kind of see-through white net. Papa was hanging orange and purple crepe-paper streamers across the entire room; not the color scheme I'd had in mind, but still, A for effort. Uncle Will was sitting on the entry floor, trying to brush the snarls out of Athena's coat as Teddy napped between her front paws.

It was working. I'd obviously inspired the family to help with the wedding.

Score!

And about flipping time!

Mom and Sarah staggered in from the back door carrying garment bags and shoe boxes. Sarah immediately shoved her hoofs into a pair of shoes, looked in the mirror on the back of the closet door and announced, "These shoes make me look squatty."

"And this dress is making me itch. I think it's made with fire ant venom," said Brandee as she scratched and tugged at the neckline.

Buzz ripped off her veil and said, "I'm just going to wear overall bibs and a coonskin cap. I could not look worse in that than I do in this veil."

Dad walked in the back door, yelling into his phone, "You can't deliver the programs in time? The name of your business is InsteePrint. What part of 'instee' don't you understand?"

Daniel, who'd followed Dad into the house, flopped on the couch and spilled a bag of napkins on the floor. He opened a book and, looking back and forth between the page and a cloth napkin, folded and rolled and twisted the material. He held it up. "Does this look like a blooming flower?"

"No," Sarah snapped, "it looks like roadkill."

"Good enough." Daniel reached for another napkin.

Papa stepped off the chair he'd been standing on to tape up crepe paper and landed on Teddy's tail, who squalled. Athena barked, jumped up and knocked over the coffee table.

Markie shook his head no when I glanced down at him. "Good man, Markie. Let's run for cover. C'mon, Sparky."

So we edged back out the door before anyone could see us and ran right into Jack, who was coming up the steps.

"Thanks for your texts, Kev. Buzz still hasn't said anything to me. I probably wouldn't have known I was getting married if not for you."

"You're okay with it? Not too sudden? Don't feel forced into it?"

"Are you kidding? I've wanted to marry Buzz since the very first time I watched her drink an entire pot of coffee."

"Congratulations. I'm sure you'll be very happy."

"Who wouldn't be with a gal like Buzz?"

"You already met Sparky, but this is Markie," I said. And, after Markie jabbed me in the gut with her head, added, "And Dumpster Assassin too."

"Buzz told me Markie's an honorary nephew." He eyed the lumpy doll; Buzz hadn't had time to bring him up to speed on the newest and most edible Spencer.

"We're handing out family memberships like crazy."

"I like that about you guys. I was an only child, and my folks didn't have any brothers and sisters. I don't have much family."

"Well, you're marrying the exact opposite of that this weekend."

He smiled, ridiculously happy to have a wedding sprung on him by a bunch of loonies.

"Hey," I said, because I am known for killing two birds with one stone, "there's probably not enough time for a bachelor party. How about we fix that right now?"

"You, me, Sparky and Markie?" I nodded. Sparky

nodded. Markie nodded. He made Dumpster Assassin nod too. "What'd you have in mind?"

"Hand-churned French vanilla ice cream with homemade hot fudge sauce, sliced bananas, slivered almonds and a tower of fluffy whipped cream."

"Extra fudge?"

"Absolutely."

I texted Dad, Daniel, Uncle Will, Goober and Papa to grab Snowphish and sneak out of the house. Then I texted JonPaul to meet us at Ruby's Shake Shack.

I'm only fourteen and this was my first stag party, but I bet it redefined the idea of a boys' night out.

Double hot fudge for everyone. Except JonPaul, who ordered a banana split, hold the ice cream and fudge, and then dumped raspberries, blueberries, pineapple, acai berries and sixteen grams of protein powder in his bowl before chasing it down with a pureed kale, spinach, wheat grass, barley grass and probiotic smoothie. Good to have you back, buddy. He was smiling and sending and receiving a lot of texts.

Jack, JonPaul, Markie and Dumpster Assassin, and Goober spent the night. I think we were dangerously close to setting an air mattress world record, but we all slept like babies.

12

The Normal Family Sacrifices to Help Each Other Out of Jams

There is nothing like a good night's sleep. More people should know that secret. I bounced to school Friday morning earlier than usual, so happy it was all I could do to keep from singing.

I was the only one.

APASTFU, which Katie and I had finished the day before, was making everyone else's life a misery.

I went looking for Katie.

I found her comforting a hiccupping and hand-flapping Connie, whose partner, Cash, was sitting on the floor with a dictionary, a thesaurus and a grammar book, trying to finish an essay question. If Connie was leaving the work to Cash, things were bad.

Katie and I gave each other a look, mutely conveying the plan. She led Connie to the girls' room and I squatted next to Cash.

"Hey, Kev," he said. "Connie and I cut it a little close; we pulled an all-nighter and now nothing makes sense because we're so tired." Cash looked up and tried to smile. It didn't go real well—it looked more like a tic. Even that made him look super handsome. Sigh.

"Well, Cash, let me take a look and see what we can do." Because I'm a nice guy, I didn't even make him promise he'd stay away from Tina forever. Thought about it, though.

I didn't have to do much more than reorganize a few sentences and paragraphs. Pressure brings out the best in some people, but not everyone. I'm one of the lucky ones.

I hadn't really noticed till now, but Crosby was super clever in the way he set up the assignments. All the questions he'd asked built on one another. If you gave a half-baked answer on Monday, by Friday you were hopelessly fouled up.

If Connie, an obsessive overachiever, had let a few things slide, I wondered about my lazier buddies.

I went looking and saw that everyone was trying to do a week's worth of work in one day.

JonPaul and Jay D. were on the steps, hunched over a laptop, banging out an answer to the final question.

I made a beeline for Tina the second I got to language arts. Although she was chewing her pencil and nervously tapping the world's most adorable left foot as she worked on her paper, she smiled and tipped her head at my buddy Wheels when she caught me looking at her.

"See if you can help him, Kev; he and Brooke ran into a few snags. I haven't got that much more to do."

Someday I'd have to remind our kids to thank me for finding them such an amazing, generous, thoughtful, kind mother.

"Where's your partner? Isn't Sean helping?"

"Sean couldn't handle the last-minute time crunch." She looked sorry for him, but I inwardly rejoiced. Sean had crumbled.

So I smiled at Tina and sat next to Wheels and Brooke Daniels, who were fifteen seconds away from stabbing each other in the forehead with paper clips.

I recalculated the figures on their ledger sheet. "Come find me when you've made the changes and we'll see if everything adds up."

Katie was across the room, getting Dash and Timmy Kurtz straightened out.

That's pretty much how the day went; Katie and I helped a few partners and then they helped others and by the end of the day every last paper was turned in on time.

It's almost like Crosby knew that was going to happen all along. Sly dog.

13

The Normal Family is an Extremely Rare Entity

I woke up to an eerie stillness Saturday morning. Silence. Freaky.

I opened my eyes and looked around; JonPaul and Goober had crashed in our basement for the second night in a row. Along with Daniel, Snowphish and me. I remembered having said good night to everyone after we got home from Daniel's hockey game; we'd all gone together.

Nobody in sight now.

I got up, did some deep breathing to get rid of the bad feeling in the pit of my stomach and headed upstairs.

I peeked into the kitchen: not a soul.

No Sarah or Buzz in the living room.

Papa and Lola were missing.

I checked my parents' room: no one.

My door was wide open—Sparky and Brandee and Uncle Will were gone.

Lucille was MIA too.

I jogged back down to the laundry room and flung open the door. Teddy was curled up in the corner, sulking. But where was Athena?

Everyone had bailed on me.

I felt like I'd woken up in one of those postapocalyptic movies where everyone disappears in some massive alien attack, leaving behind one intrepid hero who must fight for survival. Correct that: two heroes. Teddy and I would collaborate to organize a new world order.

Or at least handle the wedding. All by ourselves. I could picture our future business cards: ONE KID AND A CAT FULL-SERVICE WEDDING PLANNING.

The pressure I'd ignored all week came crashing down. I took a few minutes to alternate hyperventilating and grabbing handfuls of my hair as the list I'd dropped on the floor swirled in front of me, pulsing and throbbing in neon colors. It would have been a cool sensation under different circumstances.

I felt my heart rate accelerate and then, I swear,

stop for an ugly second. I flashed on yesterday morning at school, seeing the panicked faces as everyone scrambled to finish APASTFU. Was it only twenty-four hours ago that I'd been the calm person who helped everyone else manage their crises?

After a few more minutes of techno-pop visual hallucinations, I pulled myself together, scooped up Teddy and headed back to the kitchen.

Where I noticed lots of notes on the fridge. Everyone was running around doing wedding things.

Whoa—the pleasure of regular breathing and a steady heartbeat. Nice.

After I finished reading all the notes, I noticed that Teddy wasn't squirming to get down but hung limply in my arms.

"I know how you feel," I told my cat. "I feel dismal and hopeless when I know I'm not going to see Tina; it's hard to be in love."

So I fried us some bacon. Teddy perked up because greasy, salty, crispy pork strips make everything better.

I heard Goober and Snowphish on the front steps working on the wedding songs. And Goober tap-dancing on the front walk. Tap is his major skill. I smoothed out my crumpled list and crossed off *reception entertainment*.

I went looking for a thick black marker for Xing out everything else. A puny pencil line wasn't bold enough to convey the relief I felt knowing that people would be bringing me good news and completed tasks.

Now I could focus on the high point of any wedding day: the cake.

I'd never baked a cake before, but I'd found a great cake recipe on the Internet. I don't know why people say they're no good at cooking and baking. If you can read and follow directions, nothing can go wrong. It's almost too easy. I had the pans in the oven in a flash.

One of my favorite television shows is the bakery dude who makes super-complicated and mechanized cakes. How cool would it be if the individual layers DID something other than just sit there on the plate?

I was trying to figure out how to rig the top cake layer to explode in a sea of confetti, when I smelled something burning. Smoke billowed out of the oven and the smoke alarm started beeping. I ran over and opened the oven door, and that's when I noticed the smoke was coming from the broiler underneath the oven. I yanked it open; popcorn exploded at me. Exactly like my confetti idea.

Markie and Sparky must have put Dumpster Assassin to sleep in the broiler again.

I opened all the windows and fanned the smoke out, frantically waving a dish towel. And then I tipped Dumpster Assassin into a trash bag. I'd have to make a new popcorn-kernel baby for Markie before he realized I'd incinerated this one.

Once the smoke cleared, I checked the cake layers. They smelled like a movie theater concession stand—and not in a good way—so I tossed them in the garbage on top of Dumpster Assassin and started a new batch.

I had plenty of time; this was still a cinch. It must have been a moment like this when the phrase *piece of cake* originated.

But when I took the cakes out at the end of the baking time, they looked . . . crooked. As if I'd baked them at an angle. Oh well, that's what frosting is for.

I guess you're supposed to wait for cakes to cool before you start icing them. That wasn't in the instructions, though. Before I knew it, I was watching lopsided cake layers slide to the floor on a wave of melted frosting. JonPaul and Sam arrived as I was studying the mess. JonPaul looked at the cake on the ground and shook his head. He could see that I hoped the cake could be saved; despite the fall, the layers were still intact. Pretty much intact.

"Do you have any idea how many germs are on the kitchen floor? Even after Mrs. Spencer and I mopped and scrubbed? Let's start another."

"Third time's the charm," I agreed.

Turns out cakes are tricky. The third batch was not charmed; it was concave. Sam took one look and asked if we'd been using baking soda instead of baking powder. Who knew they were different?

We paid extra-special attention to the fourth try. The layers came out gorgeous—flat tops and golden brown. We gently tipped them onto the wire racks to cool, exhaled in relief and high-fived each other.

That's when Teddy, fed up with Athena's absence, stalked across the counter and straight through the cake layers, leaving behind gaping paw prints.

"We could just fill in the craters with icing," I offered. "No one would notice. Besides, who doesn't want a piece with a lot of frosting?"

"No!" Sam and JonPaul hollered. Then JonPaul dragged the bulging trash bag out to the garbage can next to the garage.

We were running out of time. And ingredients. How would a cakeless wedding make Tina want to use up her one and only wedding day on me?

I turned to JonPaul and saw that he was holding

Sam's hand and smiling at her. I was glad, but that wasn't going to put a cake on the table. Sam didn't panic; she shook off his hand and logged on to my laptop to research flourless and sugar-free cake recipes.

"Cake without flour is pudding, and pudding without sugar is brown slime. We're doomed." I'm not usually a pessimist, but it had been a long week, and inhaling so many burned-sugar fumes must have affected my brain.

JonPaul said, "Outside. Clear your head."

I saw Markie sitting in the bushes with Sparky and ducked under the branches to sit with them.

"Hey, Sparky, how's it going?"

"I'm not going to this wedding." He crossed his arms in front of his chest. "Miss Lola wants me to try on a suit."

"All us guys will be wearing suits."

"No. I'm going to wear my fire truck shirt."

"Okay. We'll put a tie on you, and it'll be fine."

"Are you baking, Dutchdeefuddy?" Markie pointed to my apron.

"You could call it that," I said. "Ran out of ingredients, though, so we're trying to figure out a plan B for the wedding cake."

Markie looked thoughtful. "I know!"

Most people would not take comfort in a small child's idea, but I put my faith in Markie. He's not your average four-year-old.

I followed him and Sparky into the kitchen, where Markie pushed a stool over to the pantry and grabbed a jumbo box of crispy rice cereal. "Where are the marshmallows?" He looked around.

"Marshmallows?" I asked.

"Cereal treats," Sparky answered. "We made them in school yesterday."

Brilliant. No baking necessary, no sugar or flour required. So easy the preschoolers had it covered.

Markie and JonPaul were melting marshmallows and butter and Sam and Sparky were counting out cups of cereal when the house started to get noisy again: people returning to the mother ship.

"Where have you been?" I asked Lucille and Papa, who were sitting on the couch. He held an ice pack on her arm.

Lucille answered, "I fell off a ladder, reaching to dust a soffit."

Whatever that is.

"So I took her to urgent care to get her wrist checked out," Papa said, adjusting the ice pack.

"Then we went to the farmers' market to get

flowers for the wedding. It was fun." Lucille struggled a little with the last word. I don't think she'd ever said it before.

But, man, look at the power of Kev! Papa and Lucille—becoming buddies. The jury was still out about how tight Dad and Uncle Will would be when this was all over.

Still—I rock. And Tina would love that when she got here and saw what I did.

Will had taken Athena to the dog groomer. Teddy welcomed her home with howls of joy.

I could hear Goober on the phone outside, begging Betsy to drop out of school. "You make it sound like an education is so important. What about us?"

I went out to the front steps in time to see Goober flinch and jerk the phone away from his ear. I guessed Betsy had hung up on him.

"You okay, Goob?" I asked.

"Noooooooooo!" Goober wailed.

Snowphish abandoned his practice of wah long enough to bellow at Goober: "Stop whining about your girlfriend!"

Goob and I both jumped.

"Some of us"—Snowphish jabbed his finger in Goober's face—"endure the soul-rending daily reality that our burning quest for knowledge and exploration will forever doom us to travel a solitary path. Some of us are fated to be alone throughout eternity."

"I didn't know that," Goober said.

"Of course you didn't. Because I'm about peace and healing, and I hide my sadness, channeling it into creative expression and acts of kindness. Now quit bawling, you big baby."

"Right. Sorry."

"I need help figuring out what rhymes with 'an eternal lifetime of immeasurable love and crushing financial obligation.'"

"No, dude, that's a line for an anniversary. Or a funeral," Goober said, slipping his phone in his pocket and grabbing the bongos. "How about this: 'You're more amazin' than a raisin.'"

Snowphish strummed his guitar and Goober tapped his tap shoes as they experimented. I've heard worse. And our standards weren't high.

Daniel, home from hockey practice, took one look at the floral arrangements Dad was taking out of Papa's car, and said, "What sloppy lunatic put these flowers together? They look *horrible*."

"That's what I thought," Dad said, "but I wasn't on flower duty. C'mon, son, we can fix this."

They started gathering the flowers together.

I didn't know Daniel and Dad have an eye for floral arrangements. Wonders never cease.

Jack came up the sidewalk with an armful of folding chairs. "Look! I'm helping! Just like the rest of the family!"

I have never seen a happier man. He could barely contain himself. I glanced at Jack's pickup truck. How many guests did he think we invited? He must have rented every chair in the entire state.

"That's great, why don't you, um, set them up . . . in . . . the backyard? And we'll hope it doesn't rain."

I wandered into the house and to my parents' room. I found Buzz standing in front of the mirror in her wedding dress as Lola hot-glued rhinestones on her skirt. Huh, sparkles really *do* make an outfit look special. Lola has a heavy hand with glitz. I hope everyone brings sunglasses to the ceremony or that it's an overcast day.

"So, uh, what do you think of your dress, Buzz?"

"I only wish I could wear it every day of my life! It just screams Buzz, doesn't it?"

Well, it screams something. But that isn't what a bride wants to hear, so I flashed her a double thumbs-up.

My sister was flat on her back on Mom's bed, her feet in the air, admiring her new wedding shoes. I said nothing. Better that way. We hadn't argued all week, mostly because I'd barely seen her.

Brandee came out of Mom and Dad's bathroom; Lola had already gotten to her, because it looked like a glitter factory had exploded on her dress. She rolled her eyes but smiled. "It made Lola happy," she whispered, "so don't tell her I look ridiculous, okay?"

"She'll never hear it from me."

"That was nice of you," Brandee said. "To start this whole thing with your email to Will. Thanks."

I'm pretty sure she wanted to say more, like how weird the whole family was. But clearly, she wasn't the kind of person to talk smack about her new relations. Maybe ever. That would be a nice change of pace. Brandee's a good role model.

"No worries," I said. "You were great to have offered to share your wedding with Buzz."

"My pleasure."

"I think Buzz and Jack will be good for each other. She's hyper, but she's got a good heart."

"That's what I always say about Will," she said.

We nodded, both considering the difficulty of explaining loved ones to others.

"Will made a mess of things the last time he was here, didn't he?" Brandee asked.

"Something like that."

"I'll fix it. I have what it takes to straighten him out."

"You sound determined. And not weirded out about what he might do next."

"I'm the kind of person who believes things will always work out. And, if they don't on their own, that I can find a way to make everything better so everyone is happy."

"Cool."

Lola turned to me with the glue gun and a bag of rhinestones, so I left the room quick.

I counted heads: no Mom. I hoped she was doing something food-wise, because I couldn't remember seeing that task on the fridge notes.

My phone buzzed—Katie. "Hey, I spread the word and got everyone you invited from school to sign up to bring a dish tomorrow. Catering is taken care of."

"How did you know we needed food?"

"When you said you'd run point on the wedding plans Monday, I called your mother as soon as I got home and offered to help when you ... um, well, I mean, *if* you needed assistance. She called this morning and gave me a choice of all the things that still needed to be done."

"That was amazingly cool of you. Thanks."

"What are friends for?"

Saving butt, apparently. Before I could answer, she harshed my mellow.

"Oh, hey, when are you bringing your Fine Arts Fair submission to school to set up? The fair starts tomorrow at six, you know."

As a matter of fact, I had *not* known.

Katie kept talking and I started pacing. I was starting the handful-of-hair thing again when I looked out the kitchen window and saw my family in the backyard arguing about how to arrange chairs. I saw them through a pane of glass, perfectly framed. And I knew I'd been right not to worry about the Fine Arts Fair. I had the perfect idea.

Which is so me.

14

The Normal Family Is Not Normal at All—Unless Viewed from the Inside

The double wedding went off without a hitch on Sunday.

Though it didn't go exactly as planned.

Uncle Will and Brandee didn't wind up renewing their vows in front of the whole family after all.

Because they were still at the vet having the puppies checked out. Turns out Athena didn't have a bladder infection. She'd been full of puppies.

Teddy broke the news when he streaked through the house yowling at the butt crack of dawn.

We were all awake anyway, because this is The House That Shuns Sleep, so every last one of us huddled in the laundry room and welcomed the four newest family members before Will and Brandee took them to the vet to make sure they were healthy.

And we still pulled off the ten a.m. wedding. Spencers are like that—organized overachievers who knock out litters of puppies and double weddings in the same day.

Although Will and Brandee didn't join Buzz and Jack at the altar/outdoor grill, Lola and Papa did.

The Internet rent-an-officiant showed up and asked, "Which two couples are getting married?"

"Oh, what the heck, Lola, let's do it," Papa said.

It's not the most romantic proposal there ever was and I'm not sure their marriage was legal without a license, but it would have been a shame to waste all those sequins and beads Lola had glued to her shoes and Papa's bow tie.

As Katie had promised, she, Sam, JonPaul, Tina and a dozen other friends brought food. Even Mr. Crosby came—I must have invited him on a day when I was whacked on caffeine. Daniel's hockey team, their girlfriends and Sarah's boyfriend, Doug, also showed up. Looking snappy.

Everyone who works with Jack at the bank and all of Auntie Buzz's decorating clients came. So did Betsy, even though she'd hung up on Goober the day before. I'm not sure he remembered—he didn't seem bummed. Or maybe he was just keyed up from his dance routines. Goober's tap-dancing really lightened Snowphish's depressing lyrics about the soul-sucking loss of freedom that marriage represented.

We had so many guests that Katie set up a webcam so the people seated inside the house could see the ceremony.

Tina and I exchanged a lot of Meaningful Glances during the wedding, and I'm pretty sure we were both thinking: someday this will be us. Well, I was. She may have only been thinking I looked super hot in Dad's suit, even with the safety pins holding up the pants hems. It's not normally a good look, but I made it work.

And being with Tina made it all worth it.

Weddings are magical events that bring people together.

So are Fine Arts Fairs.

After the reception, the entire wedding headed over to school, with a quick stop at the photos-while-you-wait store. I slipped my submission onto the easel labeled with my name.

My contribution was a photograph of my family.

I'd gotten the idea the day before when I saw them

through the window, and I had Katie take our picture at the reception. Technically, Katie snapped the photo, but even Michelangelo needed help carving all those statues. Collaboration is a necessity. Genius doesn't happen without a lot of support.

I finally understood what Markie had been trying to tell me about needing a line buddy: everyone needs someone who's got their back. I had a whole roomful of those people.

I didn't even take home an honorable mention. The other contestants had put in way more time and effort than me. But they didn't get to hold Tina's hand all evening like I did.

I was laughing with my friends and family and feeling Tina lean into my arm when I noticed I hadn't seen Mom and Dad in a while. I went looking and found them sitting in the car. I knew they were trying to get a little peace and quiet, but I didn't let that stop me from climbing into the backseat.

"You're welcome." I leaned back and put my hands behind my head.

"For what?" Mom sounded tired. Dad washed down a couple of headache tablets with a bottle of water.

"For bringing back family unity."

"Oh, is that what happened?" she asked.

"Yeah," I said. "And to think, it all happened because I got in touch with Will so he'd make things right with Dad."

I leaned forward, waiting for praise.

They turned to face me. Oops.

"It was a wild experience in interpersonal bonding." I grinned. They didn't smile back.

"Yeah, wild." Mom tipped her head back against the seat and closed her eyes.

This isn't how my little chats with my folks usually go. Usually, I'm the one who doesn't see things clearly and they're the ones who set me straight. Good thing I paid attention and knew how to handle this.

"That was one awesome week," I said definitively. Sometimes you need authority in your voice to get your point across.

"Really? That's what you saw?" Dad was doubtful.

"What I saw was my whole family, and some people who aren't family but should be, and a whole bunch of kids at school, helping each other out."

"Oh . . . right." Dad shrugged.

"Did you notice that Lucille is actually engaging in conversation these days? She's like a whole different person. One who likes us."

"It's a modern-day miracle, that's for sure." Mom opened her eyes.

"And she fixed the garage door opener. And Jack found a way to shake Buzz out of the garage apartment," Dad said, smiling. "Not that I haven't loved having her. All. These. Years."

"And did you notice that since Sparky started spending time with Markie, he hasn't gone near the stove?"

"I *am* grateful for that one." Mom sounded more lively.

"Papa and Lola are always cool to have around."

Dad smiled, and Mom lifted her head from the headrest.

"Goober and Snowphish have become a song-and-dance duo. Betsy and I talked Goober into staying in school and convinced Snowphish to enroll too.

"Meanwhile, Will hasn't done anything stupid or annoying or destructive or illegal the whole time he's been here."

"Yet," Dad said, but he didn't roll his eyes.

"And isn't Brandee great? I don't get how a guy like Will got someone as normal as her, but lucky for us, huh?"

Mom and Dad nodded. "She does bring out the

best in my brother," Dad said. "She may have *put* it there."

Brandee showed me that sometimes all it takes is someone who gets you to knock off your rough edges. I know how that feels. I used to think there was no word for what Katie and I are. But there is. Well, not just a word, a phrase. If Tina and I are soul mates (totally), and JonPaul and I are bros, and Markie and I are dutchdeefuddies, then Katie and I are kindred spirits.

Which is family who get each other without speaking.

I always knew that a guy like me had to get one of his big ideas right eventually. I just needed a whole lot of help from people who care about me.

I remembered a question I'd wanted to ask Mom and Dad all day. But I'd wait until later and not spoil this moment. Asking was just a formality, anyway; I'd already made my pick of the litter: a little boy dog. I named him Deacon.

Tina and I never did have the Perfect Official First Date I'd planned.

But that's okay.

Because we'll take Deacon to the dog park every day after school. And what's better than watching the sun sparkle in Tina's hair and hearing her laugh as she chases the dog and feeling her hand in mine as I walk her home?

With a vision like that ahead of me, I know there's nothing I can't achieve. Which is great, because I'm the kind of guy who's always pushing the envelope. At least where Tina's concerned.

And I have this great idea. . . .

Gary Paulsen is the distinguished author of many critically acclaimed books for young people, including three Newbery Honor Books: *The Winter Room, Hatchet,* and *Dogsong.* He won the Margaret A. Edwards Award given by the ALA for his lifetime achievement in young adult literature. Among his Random House books are *Road Trip* (written with his son, Jim Paulsen); *Vote; Crush; Flat Broke; Liar, Liar; Paintings from the Cave; Woods Runner; Masters of Disaster; Lawn Boy; Lawn Boy Returns; Notes from the Dog; Mudshark; The Legend of Bass Reeves; The Amazing Life of Birds; Molly McGinty Has a Really Good Day; How Angel Peterson Got His Name; Guts: The True Stories Behind* Hatchet *and the Brian Books; The Beet Fields; Soldier's Heart; Brian's Return, Brian's Winter,* and *Brian's Hunt* (companions to *Hatchet*); *Father Water, Mother Woods;* and five books about Francis Tucket's adventures in the Old West. Gary Paulsen has also published fiction and nonfiction for adults. He divides his time between his home in Alaska, his ranch in New Mexico, and his sailboat on the Pacific Ocean. You can visit him on the Web at GaryPaulsen.com.

Gary Paulsen is also available for select readings and lectures. To inquire about a possible appearance, please contact the Random House Speakers Bureau at rhspeakers@random house.com.

other terrific stories about Kevin

Available in hardcover from
Wendy Lamb Books
ISBN 978-0-385-74001-2

Available in paperback
from Yearling
ISBN 978-0-375-86611-1

Available in hardcover from
Wendy Lamb Books
ISBN 978-0-385-74002-9

Available in paperback
from Yearling
ISBN 978-0-375-86612-8

Available in hardcover from
Wendy Lamb Books
ISBN 978-0-385-74230-6

Available in paperback
from Yearling
ISBN 978-0-375-74231-3

Available in hardcover from
Wendy Lamb Books
ISBN 978-0-385-74228-3

Available in paperback
from Yearling
ISBN 978-0-385-74229-0